THE FINDING FREEDOM SERIES

FOURTEEN YEARS

D. RAVEN

TABLE OF CONTENTS

BLURB

MONICA ROGERS has lost her partner in life. Left alone she is scrambling with her grief, while suddenly becoming a single parent. Will there be an answer to her pain?

TREVOR CONNOR has been a patient man for Fourteen Years. Loving Monica and their daughter is all that matters. He spends his days saving everyone else around him. Will his love be enough to save himself — and the woman he loves?

*This is to all the people who think that the
love they lost means the end.*

*It doesn't.
Keep going. You're worth it.*

PLAYLIST

"The Archer" by Taylor Swift (Monica's song)
"Over and Over" by Three Days Grace (Trevor for Monica)
"Hear Me Now" by Framing Hanley (Trevor's song)
"Cinderella" by Steven Curtis Chapman (Trevor (and Paul's) song for Lacey & Lexi)
"I'm Already There" by Lonestar (Paul for his three girls)
"Officer Down" by Hannah Ellis (Monica for Paul)
"Hurt" by Johnny Cash
"Alkaline" by Sleep Token
"I Wanna Be Yours" by Arctic Monkies
"Closing Time" by Semisonic
"Only Love Can Hurt Like This" by Paloma Faith, sped up + slowed
"Someone You Loved" by Lewis Capaldi
"Here's to the Night" by Eve 6
"Angels Fall" by Breaking Benjamin
"The Only Exception" by Paramore (Monica for Trevor)
"Perfect" by Ed Sheeran (Trevor & Monica's song)

NOTE FROM
THE AUTHOR

PROLOGUE
MONICA

Before the Incident

There was a soft knock on the front door, causing Trevor to break off his sentence suddenly.

"Dammit. Hold that thought." I dropped my pen and pushed back from the rustic farmhouse table my husband had finished refurbishing for me the weekend before.

Trevor nodded, looking weary and worried. He'd stopped by after his shift at the firehouse, still in his work clothes. His blonde hair was tousled and his green eyes had bags under them. He probably wasn't sleeping well again. He'd caught word of our recent situation and wanted to check on our daughter, Lacey. Used to the chaos of our household he looked at his phone to entertain himself.

Running over to the front door, sliding in ridiculously fuzzy socks that Paul made fun of me for wearing all the time, I skidded to a stop and stood on my tiptoes. My stomach fell to my feet meeting the gaze on the other side of the window. Lowering back to the hardwood floor and staring at the door, waves of nausea rolled through me.

"Mon?" asked Trevor from behind me. I hadn't even heard him rise from his chair. Soft footsteps came closer behind me as I sensed his presence. "Why aren't you opening the door?" he laughed softly to avoid waking the three girls lying on the living room floor. They had made a nest of pillows and blankets, giggling and whispering until sleep had overtaken them.

Everything felt like I was underwater suddenly or wrapped in cotton. Finding myself shaking my head back and forth I took the first shaky breath since looking out the window.

Being married to a cop for well over ten years gave me a startling knowledge that the uniform outside on my porch at nearly midnight meant one thing. I raised a shaky hand to my forehead, my mind rushing. It wasn't his partner and I had to worry about that fact as well. That meant something horrible may have also happened to my best friend. To all of them.

The knowledge of knowing part of the news before even opening the door had my gut clenching and a soft whimper escaped my dry lips as my eyes stared at my hand on the gold shiny doorknob.

"Mon?" Trevor asked again, louder, concerned. He was right behind me, towering over me as everyone did at my height. "What the fuck?" he muttered reaching around to place his larger hand over mine. Before I could deny him, and stop this from happening, he turned it, pulling the door open with a soft creak. Unknowingly, he was forcing us to face a hell I wasn't prepared for.

"Monica," said Nick, softly. His brown eyes were kind, but shone with unshed tears. I found myself fixating on the gray starting to show in his brown hair. He was older than all of us, but still a very good friend. More a big brother figure.

Shaking my head again, I heard myself taking gasping breaths. My hand clutched the door frame as I watched his mouth begin to *move.*

That's all it took for my world to come crashing to ruin.

My knees hit the ground hard, landing on the concrete porch with a painful thud. It may hurt later when the shock over the situation had worn off. Trevor's arms went around me, his biceps clenching as he uttered a soft grunt, landing behind me. Nick lowered to a crouch in front of me, reaching out like he wanted to keep me from shattering. I was surrounded by Nick and Trevor but felt absolutely alone suddenly.

I heard them talking from somewhere far off as my heart ripped to shreds in my chest. Nick's voice was soft, explaining how it had happened and Trevor's voice broke, cursing in response. My whole body was numb but I could see myself visibly trembling like I was cold.

I couldn't breathe.

Paul.

Paul!

I took a long, audibly shaking breath in.

Then I screamed.

ONE YEAR AND
FOUR MONTHS LATER...

CHAPTER ONE
MONICA

"You ask her, Lexi."

Sighing and bracing myself, I turn around and deal with the daily sister drama occurring behind me. Lately, they chose to fight over anything and everything. The four year age difference did not help matters now that they were seventeen and thirteen.

"Ask me what?" I spoke, turning from the stove to meet the green eyes of my oldest daughter. "Lacey?" I questioned, speaking again when she hesitated to answer.

My seventeen-year-old huffed the biggest sigh known to mankind and tucked her pretty chin length blonde hair behind one pierced ear. She had gotten it cut during a weekend with her father and suddenly looked twenty-something-years-old to me. She braced her hands on the kitchen bar, countless bracelets clinking together, and hauled herself up onto it. Kicking her bare feet she wiggled, seeming to settle in for the long haul.

This had something to do with Paul then.

"Lexi is scared to ask you." Lacey began in a low voice, her green eyes flicking over to the wall hiding the stairs leading to the second floor of our ranch-style house.

"I'm not scared!" my youngest rounded the corner suddenly, her fair skin reddening in anger. Long, beautiful hair, the auburn-color of her father's, swung around her shoulders as she pointed an angry finger at her older half-sister. I raised both hands to silence them both before they could settle into a true argument.

"Lexi," I began. "You know you can ask me whatever is bothering you, sweetheart."

Her brown eyes immediately watered, moving towards the tiled kitchen floor, verifying it had to do with her deceased father. I took an audible breath, knowing that I would have to have another talk with them both about communicating with me. They were so worried about hitting a nerve with me talking about my husband that this was happening weekly now. I'd given them ample reassurances that they could talk to me about anything, whenever they needed. They felt like they were protecting me.

"It's just, the father-daughter dance is coming up in a month," she whispered in her quietest voice.

My entire body tensed, crossing my arms on the counter, I leaned over it to meet her eyes, to show her I was listening.

"I was going to ask Uncle Lucas, but I remembered he has Nat now and he'll be going with her…and Daddy…" she trailed off, tears she had been fighting streaming down her face.

I stood and held my arms open and she stepped into them, burying her face in my ratty t-shirt. My typical after-work uniform of my husband's old police academy shirt and my gray sweatpants were a regular occurrence.

"Shhh." I said softly, keeping my voice from breaking. I counted backwards from ten in my head, breathing through my nose and out through my mouth to stay calm. "We'll figure something out." My mind was racing trying to think of something and some way to fix this.

Who could I ask to take my little girl to a father daughter dance? Could I take her?

"Ask my Dad," said Lacey, quietly.

My eyes jerked up in surprise to meet hers but she was looking down at her feet. I was shocked. Usually Lacey was anything but helpful nowadays and wore her teenage angst like a badge of honor. I couldn't help being in awe at whatever had her offering this.

Trevor. My first husband and high school sweetheart. I took a deep breath. We had a good relationship and had for years now that he was clean. Usually, Lacey was selfish when it came to him and his time, and I was caught off guard at her suggestion.

"That sounds like a good idea," I choked out, finally speaking and releasing my youngest.

Lacey finally looked up at me, cheeks pink at the praise.

"Thank you for thinking of it. Would that be okay with you, Lexi?" I asked.

"Yes," she hiccuped, wiping the tears from her cheeks and smiling at her sister who predictably rolled her eyes in return.

"I'll call him later tonight and let you know what he thinks. You two, go wash your hands for dinner. No fighting." I said, shooing them out of the kitchen.

Once alone, I braced my hands on the kitchen counter and took some calming breaths, rolling my shoulders.

To be honest with myself, I was barely hanging on by a

thread. It had been one year and four months since I'd lost Paul and I still felt like he was in the house sometimes. His presence was so loud at times it was startling. I still expected him to walk around the corner from work, in his police uniform, and wrap me up in his arms.

"I miss you. How am I supposed to keep doing this alone?" I whispered out loud, my voice breaking into the silence of the kitchen. The oven timer went off and I blinked back my own tears. I hadn't allowed myself to cry in so long I was afraid if I started it wouldn't ever end. My phone beeped beside me at the same time and I picked it up, grateful for the small distraction.

Becks

Are we still on for coffee tomorrow? I have something I need to tell you.

Grinning at the message from my best friend, I peeked in at the lasagna I was making for dinner. It would need to go for a few more minutes.

Becks was like my sister. After she and her beautiful daughter entered our lives a couple of years ago, I couldn't imagine my life without her. My girls loved her daughter, Nat, like another sister and we'd gotten even closer since Becks' ex kidnapped her and we lost Paul in the process.

Yes, duh. Now I'm curious though. You can't tell me now? You know I'm impatient.

Nope. You'll have to wait, Mon. I love you.

I love you big.

I sighed, placing my phone down on the counter and looked up at the ceiling. It was way to quiet up there.

"Girls! Dinner is ready. It doesn't take this long to wash your hands!"

The thundering of feet on the stairs made me smile, yet ache inside. It wasn't that long ago Paul's voice would've been booming and laughing behind them, chasing them to the table. Lacey would've been laughing so hard she could barely stay upright, and Lexi tossed over his shoulder on the way. He could get Lacey out of her surliest moods and mediated their fighting better than I ever could.

Was I ever going to be able to go longer than five minutes without thinking of him without it killing me inside? Would the pain ever ease?

I didn't feel like I'd taken a full breath since I'd found out he had left this Earth.

I picked up the pot holders, grabbing the lasagna and green beans. I walked to the table, setting them down in the middle by the tossed salad. Lacey made a face like she was going to argue over dinner, but my quirked eyebrow must've been enough to keep her silent. I took my usual seat and worked through the slight hesitation as both girls thought they hid looks at Paul's empty place setting.

"So how was school?" my voice cut into the awkward silence.

As they both started talking over one another and I lost myself in their voices and the theatrics of middle and high schoolers, we passed food, and ate together. I believed I had done well staying strong for these two. I'd been holding it together this long. I could keep going. Falling apart and breaking wouldn't help anything. It wouldn't bring Paul back to us. I just kept putting one foot in front of the other. Never letting my girls see me fall apart except for the night we'd found out he'd left us.

I smiled and nodded, chuckling occasionally at some story they had about their day. As they were helping me wash and dry dishes while bickering again, I began bracing myself for the impending night. Lacey and Lexi would retire to their rooms for bed and another day of school tomorrow. I usually went into our room. My room? It didn't feel right referring to it in the singular. I always waited until I was sure the house was quiet and then crept to my spot on the leather couch that I hated, but Paul had loved.

I hadn't slept in our room since the night before Paul died. Everything was untouched. I dusted and cleaned in case the girls went in there but it was like a shrine frozen in time. His clothes were still on his side of the closet, his toothbrush on his side of the sink. All of his soaps and shampoo were still where he'd left them. I even had his dirty uniforms and clothes in the hamper.

No one had any idea.

Everyone thought I was doing well and moving on.

Unfortunately, I was not.

CHAPTER TWO

TREVOR

Sighing, I clicked off the television, glancing around my small, two-bedroom apartment. It wasn't much but it was clean and I took care of it. The only pictures were of my daughter Lacey throughout the years and her sister, Lexi. It was only me here anyway, except for when I had Lacey, and soon she'd be starting her senior year of high school and headed off into the world. I tried not to think about that too much.

My mind wandered to her mother. My ex-wife.

Shoving my hands through my blonde hair I turned on my side to stare at the black screen of the television. Ready for bed in my sweatpants with no shirt I let my mind drift over Monica. She was not doing well and I'd left her to her own devices for too long at this point. I couldn't begin to imagine the pain she was enduring, having lost her husband the way she did, but I'd made a promise to him that if anything were to happen I would step up to the plate. I could almost feel him screaming at me in frustration for letting it go this long. He'd rarely let his redheaded temper go, but in this instance he would've happily kicked my ass. Yet he knew her as well as I did, and Monica was a stubborn woman.

Monica and I had been high school sweethearts. Bumping into each other in the hallway one day I had taken one look at those brown eyes behind her glasses and been done. Apparently she had felt the same about a nerdy looking skateboard punk because we never looked at anyone else after beginning our relationship.

We had our fights and teenage drama, but for the most part our relationship was healthier than some adults we'd known, especially my parents. My dad had regularly kicked my ass growing up and my mother had let him.

When I'd turned seventeen, they'd both taken off one night and I'd ended up in Monica's parent's basement to finish out high school. We got married right out of high school and everything had been perfect for a couple of years.

Until my dad's ghosts had begun haunting me.

Old accomplices had enticed me to hang out with them and eventually it had led me to the same drugs my dad had turned to. I had fallen headfirst into the escape that using gave me and used it to block out the trauma from my childhood.

Monica just hadn't seemed to understand. She'd come from a happy home with two parents who doted on each other, herself, and her siblings.

Instead of opening up and leaning on my wife, I'd started doing more and more, like going to the bar and drinking until I knew she'd gone to bed.

Before I knew it, Monica was telling me she was pregnant one night and I was ashamed to admit I barely remembered because of how high I'd been. I'd managed to get clean again for a little bit. But this town was small enough that there was no way to avoid running into the same people I'd always run around with.

The stress of fatherhood and providing for a family got to me. The fear of turning out just like my father was overwhelming. I could still remember the look on her sweet face as she held our crying daughter. She'd told me they deserved better. She told me to straighten up, or get out.

I'd made the biggest mistake of my life and walked out the door.

It took overdosing and waking up in the hospital alone, realizing there was no sustenance to my life, to jar me back to reality. Yet, by the time I'd gotten my shit together and been clean for a while, Monica had met and fallen in love with Paul. A fucking cop! They graciously believed in me and let me prove myself. Let me back into their lives and have Lacey any time I wanted.

We'd grown close despite everything we'd been through and luckily there wasn't any resentment between us. I fell in love with my daughter and regretted every minute I'd spent away from her. I regretted ever picking drugs over being her father. I even got to fall in love with the daughter they had together, and also treated her like my own.

It still burned deep inside me though. The regret was bitter in my mouth and would rear its head at the damndest times. I still loved Monica and always had. What I wouldn't have given for a second chance.

The killer was, I loved Paul too. The man turned out to be like a brother to me. We even hung out for guys nights and respected each other. He talked me down off the ledge, all the time. The lure of falling off the wagon got so strong sometimes. He made himself available to me day or night. He's the one that recommended I give firefighting a try.

I finally found my passion, and the rest is history. It makes something come alive within me to save lives. The physical exertion also helps me when I think about slipping back into oblivion.

Then he was gone.

I still remember the sound of Monica's screams that night. I felt like I couldn't hold her tight enough. Like if I didn't keep my arms around her, she was going to break apart right in front of me.

I'd always wanted a second-chance but never wanted it to come this way. Paul had even sat me down once and told me that under it all he knew we still loved each other. He asked me if anything ever happened to him, not to let Monica fall into a place she couldn't come back from. He asked me to step back into her life. He asked me to take care of our daughters, and protect them all.

I sighed again, flipping onto my back. It was time to take action and keep my promise. I just knew it was going to be hell getting us both there.

Monica had been through a lifetime of hurt. First with my leaving, and then Paul being taken. I didn't even know how to initiate anything with a grieving woman, let alone one who was also your ex-wife.

Beep

I picked up my phone and stared at the screen. What are the odds?

Monica

Hey, Trevor. Are you still awake?

> Sure am. What's up? Is Lacey okay? Lexi? You?

> Everyone is fine, Trev. Can I call you?

Well this was odd. She usually kept things to text to keep anyone from prying lately. I clicked on her name to call her as my answer, sitting up on the worn couch and clearing my throat.

"Hello?" her voice was quiet, coming to me like she was sitting with me instead of across our small town of Reading, Pennsylvania.

"Mon," I replied, "What's up?"

"I have something weird to ask you and if you want to say no you can…"

"What? Anything." I replied, cutting her off.

"The school's father daughter dance is coming up in a month."

I closed my eyes, pain shooting through me, knowing how much that had to hurt her and Lexi. I could remember taking Lacey when she was that age. The memories it had created and what it meant to those girls to have that experience.

"Lexi was going to ask Lucas, but remembered he has Nat now…"

"I'll take her." I butted in. "Let me know the date, time, and the color dress she's wearing." I spoke gruffly.

"Trev," Monica's voice broke.

"I'd do anything for that little girl." I continued. "She's like a daughter to me, and she's my actual daughter's sister. You never have to worry about asking me anything regarding things like this."

"Thank you." she whispered, sniffling.

"Mon, are you okay? Do you need to talk?" I asked, trying to bridge that wall she'd erected around herself.

"I'm fine. Actually. I think I hear Lacey. I'll have her call you in the morning. Thanks. Bye." And she was gone.

I sighed, tossing my phone onto the low coffee table.

Shaking my head, I spoke out loud.

"Keep running, Monica. I'm coming after you and you're going to let me help."

CHAPTER THREE
MONICA

"You beat me here." I said, sliding into the creaky booth of the cafe across from my best friend. This place was so old, my parents had dated here when they were young. Styled to look like a fifties diner, it had turned into more of a hometown Starbucks under the fifth generation of owners.

Becks smiled at me, looking radiant as always. My eyes glanced over at her, taking stock. She looked like she was doing well, all those raven curls thrown up in her typical messy bun, not unlike my own. Her dark eyes narrowed at me behind her glasses.

"Stop giving me the once over, Monica." she laughed in her husky voice. "Everything is fine."

I tilted my own brunette head with some sass, pushing my glasses up my nose and leaning forward.

"I can't help it." I said. "Ever since everything happened I still expect you to be hurt in some way." I said, my voice was smaller than it had started out.

Her eyes softened and she put her hand on top of mine, squeezing reassuringly.

"I feel the same way about you." She said pointedly. "Open up Monica." She said suddenly. "Talk to me. I know things are hard right now and you're hurting. You absolutely refuse to talk to anyone-"

"Stop." I cut her off, alarmed. Sitting back in the booth. I picked up a plastic menu and hid behind it, clearing my throat. "This isn't about me right now. I'm fine. What were you going to tell me?"

Becks sighed and I could sense her stare through the menu.

"Fine. I'm letting you get away with this one more time, but eventually we're going to talk, Monica."

I waved her off, dropping the menu and picking up my mocha latte she'd ordered, to take a sip.

"Mmmmmmm." It tasted divine.

"I have some news," she began, still staring at me.

I glanced up at her, taking another sip.

"Mmhmm?" I hummed questioningly.

"I had a doctor's appointment yesterday."

I slammed my mug down, the liquid sloshing over the side. "Are you okay?"

Becks threw her head back and laughed, tears filling her eyes as I looked at her concerned.

"Jesus, Monica," she said. " I'm fine. I'm just pregnant."

I gasped and covered my mouth. "Pregnant?" I shrieked, drawing the eyes of several patrons.

"Shhhhh!" She giggled and nodded, "Two months along. I even know the gender. But I'm not telling anyone because we have a party planned. You're the only person, other than Lucas, that knows that I'm pregnant. I'm the only one that knows the gender. I couldn't keep it from you any longer. We just wanted to wait a bit to make sure everything was okay. Because I'm old and shit." She snorted and laughed, shaking her head.

"Oh, fuck off. You're not old, Becks. Oh my God. I'm so happy for you!" I said, tears slipping down my face. "A baby." I whispered.

"Tell that to my doctor. Labeling me a geriatric pregnancy." She scoffed, sipping her tea.

I thought it was weird she hadn't ordered coffee.

"It wasn't planned, obviously. Lucas was fine with Nat being his child, but I guess the universe had other ideas." she smiled, sliding an ultrasound picture across the table. "I'm drinking decaf for a while," she grimaced.

"Oh my, God," I whispered again, fingers tracing the image. "Paul would have been elated." I blurted out the first thing coming to my mind at the moment.

Becks' hand covered mine again, her own eyes welling up again. "I know," she whispered. "Lucas actually got very emotional when we found out. After the initial panicked look and sitting there in silence when I showed him the test of course. His instinct was to call Paul before he..... Mon, are you sure you don't want to talk?"

"No. Absolutely not." I said sternly. "This is happy news and a happy occasion. I don't need to bring anyone down."

Becks accepted the ultrasound back from me and stared solemnly. "You wouldn't be bringing anyone down, Mon." she said. "I feel like with all my happy news and occasions, the engagement, wedding, and now this? I don't want you to feel like your grief has been brushed aside."

"Becks," I shook my head, "Your happiness, and your life being amazing, is keeping me afloat. You and my daughters, of course. Knowing how ecstatic Paul was for Lucas to find someone finally. He adored you. Oh my God, I'm going to be an aunt!" I exclaimed.

She laughed tearfully and brushed her face, wiping the wetness away with the sleeve of her sweatshirt. "I'm hungry." she added. "I'm always hungry lately. I was so sick with Nat the whole pregnancy that this is weird."

"Lucas' genes must be strong with this one." I said wisely, grabbing the menu again. "Let's eat then! I can't have my little niece or nephew hungry, can I?"

Becks leaned back against the red, leather booth and placed a hand on her stomach. Quirking my eyebrow, I laughed at her.

"You weren't kidding when you said you were hungry!" My eyes slid down to the plates in front of her. I didn't think I'd ever seen my friend eat that much food.

"I'm trying to watch it and only allow myself to pig out on breakfast twice a week." she replied, sheepishly. I watched her cheeks pinken and berated myself a bit, knowing she'd heard horrible things from her ex about her weight.

"I'm just kidding, Becks. You're growing an entire human. If they have Lucas' genes, they need all the calories to get that big." I joked, referencing her six-foot-six powerhouse of a husband.

Lucas had been Paul's best friend and partner on the force. When he'd met and fell in love with Becks, Paul and I had been so thrilled that he'd finally found an outlet for all the love he had to give. I just regretted that Paul wasn't around to see the fruit of our efforts pay off.

Becks' phone chimed, and I watched her pick it up as I sipped my latte. She rolled her eyes and started putting things in her purse.

"Lucas likes to check in on me even more than usual now." she explained as I also began gathering my things from the table and throwing them into the tote by my side. Sunglasses, cell phone, glasses case, a girl could never be too prepared.

"Thank you for meeting me for breakfast, and to talk," said Becks standing up and smiling down at me. I stood up with her and still had to crane my head a bit. I was five-five but Becks was five-foot-ten. I was used to having to look up at the people around me anyways.

"Oh, stop. You know I'd meet you for every meal, every day if I could." I wrapped my arms around her in a hug.

"I wish we could do that." she responded, hugging me back.

"I'm sorry if I've been a downer this year." I whispered, suddenly.

"Mon," began Becks. "I'm not just here for the sunshine days. I'm here for everything."

"I know. I just feel like I've only been the storm the last year and a half."

"With good reason," she scolded. "You lost your husband, Monica. You won't talk to anyone about it. I can text Lucas back and we can chat longer-"

"No." I said slightly panicked. "I'm okay. I just felt like I needed to say thank you."

"You don't." She looked at me skeptically. "I love you."

"I love you too." I replied, watching her turn and walk out of the diner. I sighed, glancing down at my phone to see the time. It was summer so I was off work and had the whole day ahead of me.

Being a receptionist for the local school had its perks. I basically had half of June and all of July, off work. Lacey was with her friends at the pool, while Lexi and Nat were at a volleyball summer camp for the day.

Trevor

Hey, Mon. Are you busy right now?"

My eyebrows lowered at the text coming through my phone. Trevor and I talked regularly but it was rare to hear from him two days in a row. Even if I'd been the one to message him last night. Ever since Paul had passed away, he'd been checking in more frequently. He used the guise of Lacey to do so, but I knew he was worried about me and Lexi as well.

Nope. Just had a girls brunch with Becks. I have the whole day ahead of me.

Can you come over so we can talk?

I guess, is everything okay?

Yeah, I've just been meaning to have a conversation with you for a while. No time like the present.

Be there in thirty.

Tossing my phone in my tote, my mind started racing on what could be happening with my ex-husband. I wondered if he'd finally started seeing someone. He had only briefly dated people since we'd divorced, after he got his life together. I was so proud of him for being clean and holding down his job as a fireman. He had a new zest for life that I hadn't seen since high school, when I'd met him. My heart grew warm in my chest. He had grown into a good-looking man and was back to being healthy. He actually could be in one of those fireman calendars for fundraisers. I snorted to myself thinking about it. I wouldn't be surprised if a new woman in his life was what he was about to tell me about.

CHAPTER FOUR
TREVOR

"Fuck!" I muttered, grabbing a towel to wipe the toothpaste from the mirror. Glancing into my bedroom I saw I had ten minutes before Monica had said she'd be here. I didn't know why I felt so nervous. We saw each other regularly.

Just knowing I was about to start the process of trying to win her back was putting my stomach in knots. I backed up, looking at myself in the mirror. I had packed my six-foot-three frame with muscles since becoming a firefighter. I had also covered myself with tattoos and gotten a couple piercings in my moments of stupidity, grateful they still looked good.

The eyebrow piercing looked so natural it would be weird to remove it at this point. The other piercing wasn't something just anyone could see.

I'd left my blonde hair shaggy on top, having never quite grown out of the skater-boy haircut from high school and my younger years.

"Jeans and a shirt should be fine." I said to myself. "Dude. Pull yourself together. It's just a conversation."

Walking out of my bathroom, and through my bedroom, I entered the main living area of my apartment.

"Coffee," I said to myself, going into the kitchen to prepare a pot. Monica had been addicted to the stuff in high school and never looked back. I'd never quite developed the taste, preferring my soda and energy drinks.

"Just going to talk about how she's doing today, it's not like you're going to confess your undying love for her." I groaned at the thought, bending to set my head in my hands, with my elbows on the beat up countertop of the small kitchen. I was nervous as hell. There was no denying it. I wanted to offer her an ear to listen or a shoulder to cry on. I knew she was missing Paul. I knew she was struggling to do everything alone. Monica had never been the type to ask for help from anyone. It was something we'd fought over and had made me feel illogically useless in our young relationship.

Not only did I have shitty role models growing up, but I'd suddenly had the stress of a wife and baby. All the expectations had just crowded around me and I hadn't been enough or felt like enough. I'd convinced myself that she could do better and that Lacey needed someone different in their lives. I was just a constant disappointment.

Throwing caution to the wind was the theme of the day. I was still in love with my ex-wife. I had been too late getting my shit together back then, but I had it together now.

Standing, I grabbed my water bottle, chugging some down. I just wanted to make the moves slight. Paul wouldn't have wanted her to not move on. He'd told me as much when he asked me to step back in. He'd known Monica had a stubborn streak a mile long.

Monica was loyal to a fault. She was likely to lock herself in her house and never move on. She was only thirty-eight. She had so much life ahead of her. Paul didn't want her to play the widow for the rest of her life.

I didn't ask for this second chance. I never wanted it to happen this way. Paul was one of my best friends. I gripped the counter again, knuckles whitening. I'd waited a year and a half. I could test the waters. If she balked or it went too horribly, I could wait longer. I'd been waiting so long already.

My head jerked up at the knock on my front door and I hurried towards it, tripping over my own feet and stumbling a little to answer it.

"God, you're a dumbass," I muttered to myself. I stared through the peephole of the old, brown, apartment door. Pretty sure this place hadn't been renovated since the nineteen-nineties.

There she was. Brunette hair thrown up on top of her head, nose scrunched under her glasses as she checked her phone. I looked her over, knowing she couldn't see me. Leggings, a baggy t-shirt, and sneakers completed her usual summer uniform. She was fucking gorgeous. I watched her sigh and look up again, moving to knock a second time.

Gripping the door handle, I swung it open, meeting her wide eyes, hand raised to knock, and grinned.

"Hey, Mon. You look good." I stepped out, hugging her briefly.

"Hi, yourself," she laughed softly, returning the affection.

I ushered her into the apartment, gesturing towards the empty recliner or couch. The room already felt brighter with her in it.

She smelled like coffee and lavender soap. She perched on the couch and looked out the window at the oak tree that blocked most of the view.

"That tree is going to fall right into this apartment someday," she said, head swiveling to look at me.

"Trust me. As a fireman, I know this." I chuckled, sitting on the other side of the sofa. "Try telling that to my stubborn ass landlord."

Nodding, Monica's eyes moved over me, seeming to take stock.

"So," she began, "What did you need to talk to me about?"

I shrugged my shoulders and leaned back against the couch, trying to relax.

Monica sniffed, looking towards the kitchen.

"Is something burning?" she asked suddenly.

The coffee.

Jumping back up I ran into the kitchen to see smoke coming from the burner under the pot. I apparently needed to learn how to make coffee again. I hadn't done it for years, since living with her. I'd only bought the new machine yesterday, just for this moment.

"Dammit," I muttered. "Don't tell anyone about this. Ever. I'll never live it down if the guys at the station hear about it."

Monica was snorting on the couch.

"Since when do you make coffee anyway?" she asked.

I stalled, panicked. I didn't want her to know I'd bought it just for her.

"I'm trying to break the energy drink habit." I blurted out.

"Finally." she praised, cheeks pink from laughing at my spectacle. "Those things are horrible for you."

"Yeah, yeah." The brown sludge in the pot was mocking me and I sighed, glaring down at it.

"Trevor."

My green eyes shot up, meeting Monica's beautiful brown ones.

"Don't worry about the coffee. I had two lattes at brunch." she shook her head at me.

"Right. Of course you did." I tossed the pot into the sink and unplugged the machine, walking back over to the couch sheepishly.

"I just thought I'd ask you over to see if we could talk about things." I began, sitting back down on my side of the sofa, stretching an arm across the back of it.

Monica's eyes narrowed at me.

"Are you seeing someone?"

I choked.

"What?" I stuttered. That was not where I saw this conversation going.

"I just thought that may be what you wanted to talk to me about. You've dated off and on for years but never committed. You seemed so serious about it all. I thought you were telling me about a new woman you were bringing into Lacey's life."

"No." I sat up straighter, shaking my head. "There's no one."

"Oh…okay?" she looked confused now. "What is it then? Are you sick?" she looked slightly panicked now.

"No. Monica. I just wanted to tell you that I'm here for you. I'm here to talk to if you need someone. Not just something for the girls like last night. I'm here for you, hon." I said.

She stilled, looking at me intently for a minute. Her eyes were filled with tears that she was rapidly trying to blink back. I continued staring at her seriously.

"I'm fine." she said, looking down at her lap where her hands lay, fingers intertwined nervously.

I scooted closer, just slightly, and reached over, laying my hand over hers, stilling them.

"Mon," I said softly.

Then she broke. I didn't even know how to describe the sound that came out of her. It was like the night we'd learned Paul had died. Only this time it wasn't a scream. It was just a broken, tired sob and she curled in on herself.

"Monica," I said again, scooting up against her now, wrapping her in my arms. I'd just let her cry for now. I wondered how long it had been since she'd actually let herself.

"I'm not okay," she blurted out. "Everyday people ask me if I'm okay. You're like the sixth person today. People that know Paul or me, or of Paul and me. They ask twenty-four-seven if I'm okay. I'm not. Why would I be okay? What do they expect me to say? I have a seventeen-year-old and thirteen-year-old I'm suddenly raising alone. I'm expected to move on, daily. I feel like with everything happening in my best friend's life I can't ask for help. I can't sleep. I can't sleep in my bed-"

"Whoa, slow down." I'd known she was holding a lot in but this broken, sob-filled monologue was taking me off guard.

She swiped at her tears, angrily, even as she kept sobbing and continued.

"Lucas and you mowed my lawn for a few weeks but I felt so guilty over it. You all have lives and I felt like I couldn't keep asking. Did you know I had to search YouTube to learn how to run the mower? I had to YouTube how to fix a leak in the shower the other day too. Then there's the girls, they used to go to Paul for so much more than I realized. Now they feel like they can't talk to me about anything involving him or I'll go off. Like some timebomb waiting to explode."

I squeezed her tighter, letting her rant. *Jesus.*

"I haven't even slept in my own bed since the night before Paul died. I can't. I move to the couch after the girls lay down for the night. I can't go through his clothes. I can't ask anyone to help me. I feel like everyones moved on and I'm frozen in time. Some days are good and I feel like I could start trying to move on if I had someone there to help me, but the next day I'm terrified of that thought process. Of getting rid of the way things were and forgetting him. Like it's a slap in Paul's face. It was Monica and Paul for fourteen years, Trev."

She finally stopped, sobbing into my shoulder, as I just stared down at the top of her messy bun. That was a lot more information than I thought she'd give me. I hadn't expected her to open up so thoroughly to me although I was glad she had. I squeezed my arms tighter in what I hoped was a comforting hug.

Monica's sobs were becoming hiccups and she was practically laying against me. I cleared my throat and tried to speak softly.

"Mon. Paul wouldn't have wanted this for you. He even told me that at one point."

She jerked back, straightening and staring at me. Her glasses had water on them and she was so adorably disheveled I was having trouble focusing.

"What do you mean?" she hiccuped. I watched her hands nervously fall to her lap. Her fingers found the sapphire ring that Paul had left instructions for Lucas and Becks to give her if something had ever happened to him. His ashes were a part of it and she never took it off since she'd gotten it for Christmas.

"Paul used to talk to me about his job and the dangers." I shrugged, sitting up with my arms on my knees. "He didn't want me to let you live your life alone with those girls if anything ever happened to him." I continued, keeping it basic.

"You're thirty-eight years old, Monica. No one deserves to live their life alone. The things you just told me? Any one of us would've helped you with. You're not a burden at all. You don't have to do it alone. Becks and Lucas would feel horrible if they knew you weren't going to them with things. Especially Becks. She's been berating herself for all her happy events, according to Lucas, because she knows you've been holding back and not letting things out. But, even if you felt you couldn't go to them with things. Mon, You have me, what about me?"

My eyes swung to hers.

"You should know that I am here. I will always be here, Monica. We used to be married. We have a damn daughter together. Do you need a leaky shower fixed? I can do it. Do you need someone to cry on? I'm your guy. You need someone to help you go through Paul's things? Tell me when, sweetheart."

Her eyes started watering again at my words, and she removed her glasses with shaky hands, tears trailing down her flushed cheeks.

"I'm just so scared. I've been so scared." she broke again.

I had her back in my arms, rubbing her back soothingly.

"Well. Now I know, and you don't have to be." I promised.

CHAPTER FIVE

MONICA

Sighing, I took a healthy drink of my coffee. Instead of making it at home this morning, I'd splurged and gotten us all iced coffee at the shop in town. Lexi liked to think she was drinking coffee at least. Hers was more glorified chocolate milk at this point.

It made me chuckle to watch her swirl her cup around, watching her older sister to see just how she did it. My oldest was suddenly drinking nearly black coffee and it made me want to gag. She'd surpassed me on that front. She asked for a splash of cream and drank it like it was the best thing she'd ever tasted. Trevor's was in the fridge waiting for him, since he'd told me the other day he had given up the energy drinks.

We'd planned this Saturday to go through my bedroom finally and hopefully get some closure. Trevor was coming over to help if things got too rough for me. A stable presence for the girls.

When I sat the girls down a couple of days ago after dinner,

I'd finally laid everything out for them.

"What's going on?" Lacey was eyeing me warily from her spot on the couch. Already dressed in the sleep shorts and tank top she preferred for bed. Her green eyes peeked out at me from the facial mask she was wearing as she drew her legs up to sit criss-cross.

When had she gotten so adult-like?

Lexi was fidgeting next to her, wearing one of Paul's academy t-shirts. She'd asked for a few of them to rotate as sleep shirts. They comforted her and I let her take her pick. Lacey had taken a couple as well, but I never saw her actually wear them. I had a feeling she was sleeping with them like a blanket at night. I wasn't going to pry and ask. We were all handling our grief in different ways.

"Nothing is wrong." I shook my head at my oldest, crossing my own legs in the recliner. I was wearing my typical sweatpants and sweatshirt that I wore to bed. I always get so cold at night lately, and there was no body heat to keep me warm anymore.

"I just think I need to come clean to you about a few things. I know it's been rough since your dad passed." I started, speaking softly, trying not to notice the way Lexi's eyes immediately filled with tears.

"I've not been handling it as well as I could be." I started speaking softly.

I laid out everything for them, within reason for their ages. The fact that it was too lonely in that room. I had been sleeping on the couch where they sat right now every night. Lacey looked concerned and worried while Lexi just silently cried.

"I haven't handled my grief like I should've in front of you two. You all shouldn't be tip-toeing around me, scared to bring your dad up because I may cry. It's okay to cry."

The more I'd spoken, it seemed weights were dropping off both my girls' tense shoulders. I regretted letting it go on this long. My oldest's eyes had sparked when I'd mentioned her father had been the one to finally cause me to break and admit some of this stuff. When I'd suggested clearing out my bedroom, they'd been eager to help. They'd taken what they wanted and what Paul would've wanted them to have in the weeks following his funeral.

Everything else I didn't want or need had been sold or donated. It was literally our bedroom. Frozen in time because I was scared of forgetting the man I'd been married to. I could see the irrational part of that. There was no way I'd ever forget such a big presence in my life. Especially when our youngest looked so much like him.

"When's Dad supposed to be here?" Lacey's voice startled me. I hadn't noticed her coming up behind me in my musings. Glancing at my phone, I noted the time.

"Any minute now—" I answered right as the doorbell rang.

Lexi was running towards the door, always eager to see Trevor, and I heard her excited voice greet him as she shook the ice cubes in her drink again.

"Lex!" Trevor exclaimed "Are you drinking a coffee? When did you get so big on us?"

"I'm thirteen." I heard my daughter giggling and responding as they walked closer into the kitchen.

My eyes narrowed, taking in the energy drink clutched in his hand.

"I thought you'd given those up?" I pointed at it, tilting my head and staring at him, when I realized he looked good. Low-slung, gray sweats with a black shirt covering his muscular chest and arms. I had no business checking out my ex-husband like this. In the house I'd lived with my deceased husband for fourteen years. Shaking my head I met his eyes again.

His brow was quirked and he had a smirk on his face, like

he'd caught me noticing him. I felt my cheeks heat, knowing they were pink now.

"What?" he asked, distracted from my question.

"The energy drink. You told me the other day you'd started drinking coffee?" I spoke again, raising my own eyebrow in response.

His eyes grew big and he shook his hair off his forehead.

"Right..." he seemed to be at a loss for words.

Something clicked in my head. This man.

"Trevor. Please tell me you did not buy a brand new coffee pot just because I was coming by your apartment for a conversation." I laughed at the ridiculousness as Lacey watched the interaction intently. Lexi had already wandered off, back to her television show.

Trevor shrugged, "You know I'd do anything to make you happy, Mon," he stated quietly.

He elbowed Lacey gently. "Hey beautiful." He slung an arm around her shoulders drawing her close even as she tried to pull away, obviously too cool for her dad. He growled and kissed her forehead anyway as she rolled her eyes at him.

"Dad. So uncool." she turned on her heel, stalking out of the room, trying to stomp her bare feet. Her chin-length hair was up in a sassy ponytail today.

Trevor shook his head, watching her walk out of the room.

"When the hell did she become an adult?" he asked, turning his gaze on me.

I snorted, still overwhelmed at the thought of him buying a coffee pot, for one conversation.

"We blinked, Trev."

He nodded, letting his eyes run over me from head to toe.

Was he checking me out this time? What was going on?

"Anyway," I stammered. "Are you ready to get to work? I was thinking of completely stripping everything in the bedroom and bathroom. All decor and bed things. I think a complete remodel is in order, decoration wise. So it feels new, like my own space."

The man smirked at me again, like he knew something I didn't and he knew I was changing the subject. I chose to ignore him and walked past him and up the stairs, yelling at my children to meet me and Trevor in the bedroom.

Lacey and Lexi were fighting, yet again. I'd told them they could take decorations from my bathroom and redo the one they shared together, if they wanted.

Lexi liked the barbie pink bathroom the way it was and Lacey was insistent they needed something more grown up.

I could feel my oldest losing it as the other grew more and more whiny. Trevor had frozen at this point, watching the interaction in amusement.

I threw my hands up, tired of the bickering.

"Okay." I said, crossing my arms and using my best mom voice. "Lacey, if you want to move into the guest bedroom that has a bathroom connected, then do it and decorate it how you want. But," I raised my eyebrows as my oldest started to celebrate prematurely,"you have to be okay with giving that up for guests when they're here." I continued.

"Yes! Yes! Yes!" she sprinted from the room, presumably to start moving furniture and bathroom items to her new space.

Lexi pouted after her.

"And why the face? I thought this was a good compromise?" I asked my youngest.

"It is. I like how my bathroom is. But she gets a whole new room and everything-"

Covering my face with my hands, I sighed. Children.

"Okay. Move to Lacey's old room.." I said exasperated. Now Lexi squealed and took off excitedly.

"And there better not be any yelling!" I hollered after her as Trevor chuckled from across the room.

Everything was bare bones. The bed stripped to the mattress and box springs, curtains down. All the decor and old bedspread and sheets were bagged and ready to be donated to the local center for abused women in recovery from bad relationships.

Becks and I volunteered there together every other Saturday because it was a cause near and dear to her after everything she'd been through.

Paul's side of the closet was empty now. Shoes and old clothes are going to be donated as well. I'd kept a few shirts and hoodies for myself. Even a pair of sweatpants.

The bathroom was empty. I'd kept a bottle of his cologne and moved it to my side. The morning had been emotional and hard, but it felt lighter here somehow. I was sad. I was still grieving. But I felt like I could start healing now, too.

I had one drawer on Paul's nightstand to go through and sat cross legged in front of it as Trevor started carrying things downstairs to his truck.

Taking out a few books and Paul's reading glasses I noticed an envelope peeking out of a magazine at the bottom. Narrowing my eyes I reached in and drew it out.

It had one word scribbled on the front. My name. Feeling

breathless, my heart rate sped up and my anxiety spiked. My mind spiraled on what it could contain. I hadn't gone through anything after the funeral. I hadn't known this was there. I heard myself breathing shakily as I ran my fingers over his handwriting.

I opened the unsealed flap and drew the paper out, recognizing more of his handwriting, tears filled my eyes.

Monica,

If you're reading this, then the worst has happened and I've been taken from you. I want you to know that, while I love my occupation, this has always been my biggest fear. I'm not scared of dying. I don't fear what comes after, baby. I am terrified of leaving you in the devastation I know you'll feel. I'm petrified of leaving Lacey, who I've come to love as my own flesh and blood. And, the spitfire we created together in Lexi. If I'm not there to protect my girls, who will?

Logic says Trevor. Nick. Lucas. They'll all step up. If you'll let them. Don't look at me that way. You're stubborn. Let them in, baby. Don't wall yourself away. We loved epically. We got to experience what some people never do. You are my North Star. You're my reason. You're my everything. It hurts. I know it hurts so badly. But, I pray that this letter is something you find soon after I'm gone, so that you know it's okay, Monica.

It's okay to cry for me. It's okay to be devastated and grieve. But it's not okay to sit there in it, baby. I want you to live. I want you to find love again. You are not the type of woman that should ever have to do life alone. I am not the type of man that would ever expect you to play the martyred widow for the rest of your life. I don't know who he will be. I have my suspicions. But ultimately the choice will be yours. Fate has to decide somewhat.

Let people in. Especially Trevor. He will love you with a ferocity that can only be matched by me, baby. The way that man looks at you. I know he has regrets. I love him like a brother now. I respect him. I am doing everything but shoving you at him and together. But if he wanted a chance, take it. He was your first love. He loves Lexi like his own. Like I love Lacey. I couldn't imagine anyone better.

Stop scowling at me like that. You'll get wrinkles.

Monica. I Love You. With every single fiber of my being. It's killing me to even write this. But I know I need to. Because I know you. This job is dangerous. We never know what could happen. I hope you never have to go through things to find it. But if you do, you need to know all of this. I'll always love you.

If there's a way, I'll be using it to be with you all always. I LOVE YOU, Monica Rodgers. I love our babies. Be happy. For them. For ME. Fall in love again.

I love you. I love you. I love you.

Paul <3

Sobbing, I pressed the papers with his handwriting to my chest, taking deep gasping breaths. That man. He'd had everything in order. He knew me inside and out. He knew I would sit in this grief. I *was* stubborn. Here I was a year and a half after he was gone, just finding this. Just feeling one more miniscule bit of closure.

"Monica?" I startled at Trevor's concerned voice behind me. Folding the paper and putting it back in the envelope, I shook my head, wiping my tears away with shaking hands.

"Are you okay?" he was standing over me, behind me, from where I sat in front of the nightstand. I looked up at him, tilting my head back.

"Not quite. But I'm getting there a little more each day."

CHAPTER SIX

TREVOR

Looking in my rearview mirror, I fidgeted with my hair again. It looked fine and I didn't know why I was so nervous. I was taking a middle-schooler to a father-daughter dance. Yet, it was a grieving middle-schooler who was my biological daughter's half-sister.

Oh, and I was in love with her mother, my ex-wife. I shook my head and reached over, picking up the little wrist corsage that I had bought for Lexi. Monica had called me a couple weeks ago to let me know she'd chosen a blue dress, in memory of Paul. I went with the theme, wearing a matching blue shirt under my suit coat. Looking at the corsage I had to clear my own throat.

Tiny blue roses with baby's breath kept it simple, but I'd had the florist add a couple of charms. One was Paul's badge number and another held a small picture of him. He'd been so excited about his turn at a dance like this with Lexi. Years ago when I'd picked Lacey up he'd jumped around like a kid himself, taking pictures and telling Lexi they'd do it some day.

I sighed and stepped out of the truck, shutting the door behind me. I hoped I'd made it special for Lexi, and there wouldn't be too much pain. I wanted her to have fun too. A couple of the guys from the police station had daughters around the same age and were taking them as well. They'd all promised to ask for a dance for Paul's memory. Lexi had no idea. Monica had cried when I'd told her and made me promise to get pictures of all of them.

Ringing the doorbell, my own daughter opened it, leaning against the door jamb, giving me the up and down.

"Do I pass inspection, ma'am?" I turned, holding my arms out.

Lacey snorted and shook her head at me.

"Thank you for doing this for mom and Lexi," she said softly.

"You know I'd do anything for them, and you." I stated, reaching out and tapping the end of her nose, even as she scrunched it and tried to back away. *Teenagers.*

"I know. It's just been hard." she broke off, staring down at her toenails, that I now noticed were painted black. *What happened to bubble gum pink?* I kept getting the reminders that she wasn't my baby anymore.

Turning, she guided me into the house.

"Mom and Lexi are upstairs finishing the final touches" she used her fingers in sarcastic air quotes. "Mom ordered us chinese and is going to let me pick the movie," she threw herself down onto the leather couch, pulling a fluffy blanket over her legs, left bare in her pajama shorts.

"That'll be fun." I encouraged, sitting in the recliner and crossing an ankle over my knee.

"I hope she'll let me get something rated PG-13 or R since Lexi is going to be gone."

I raised an eyebrow at her.

"What? I'm old enough." she scowled now.

"I keep forgetting. I keep seeing that bald-headed baby they handed me so many years ago."

"Dad!" she exclaimed, throwing a pillow at me.

"She's ready." Monica's voice came from behind us and I stood again. My ex-wife was adorable. Wearing pajama pants and a sweatshirt two times her size, hair thrown in her usual style, she grinned at me.

"Thank you so much for doing this, Trev. She's so excited."

"Always." I told her.

"Come on down, Lex." Monica yelled up the stairs.

Lexi walked down slowly, a faint blush to her cheeks. It made me choke up a little bit, realizing how big she was getting too.

Her blue dress was princess-like and glittery, everything a new teenager could want. Monica had curled her hair and put it in an elegant updo. Makeup was minimal and glittery. I noticed the small diamond necklace she was wearing was one I'd given Monica when we'd been dating in high school.

Stepping to the bottom of the stairs to meet her, I took her tiny hand and bowed slightly.

"Lexi, you look stunning." I said.

Blushing and giggling she twirled in her sparkly, silver, ballet flats as her mom sniffled and snapped pictures on her phone.

"I had this made special for you, kiddo," I said softly, handing her the corsage container.

Lexi looked at it confused, as Monica giggled.

"You put it on your wrist, dork." Lacey said, peering over the back of the couch, watching.

"Lacey." Monica and I scolded at the same time.

"What? Jeez. Sorry. You look pretty, Lex."

Lexi preened under her older sister's praise, Monica stepping over to help her open the container.

I knew the moment that mother and daughter saw the charms I'd added to it. Lexi's tiny fingertips brushed over them gently, the glittery polish on them reflecting the light.

"Trev…" Monica's voice was soft and tear-filled.

"I just wanted to do something special. He's here with us." I said, stepping forward and sliding the piece onto her little wrist. "Figured you all could dry it out and save it. Or I can buy a chain to put the charms on for a bracelet." I was rambling, nervously.

"It's perfect, Uncle Trevor," whispered Lexi, "Thank you."

"You're welcome, Squirt." I replied.

"You two better get or you'll be late for the ball." joked Monica, still sniffling.

After posing for a couple more pictures and joking about curfews, Lexi and I headed out to her first dance, promising her mother again that I'd take all the pictures.

Riding to the school in my big truck, Lexi squirmed excitedly beside me.

"Nervous at all?" I asked, while some pop princess the teenage girls were obsessed with crooned on the radio.

"No!" she exclaimed, smiling over at me. "I'm so excited. Thank you for taking me, Trevor."

"You girls have to stop thanking me for this." I laughed, pulling into the school parking lot. "I'd do anything for all of you."

Helping her down from the passenger side, she gripped

my big hand as we stepped into the gym. It looked like they'd changed things since prom. It looked like some sort of Hollywood level production.

I felt fucking old.

"LEXI!" Nat's voice screeched as her tiny body barreled into her friend, Lucas walking up shaking his head behind her.

"Hey, man," he nodded at me. "Nice suit."

"Back at you." I said, taking stock of him. "Who would've thought we could clean up so well?" I asked.

"The things we do for love." he muttered, tugging on the collar of his pink dress shirt.

"Real men wear pink." I affirmed, watching Lexi and Nat jump up and down, chattering excitedly. The blue tulle of Lexi's dress stuck to the pink glitter of Nat's reminding me of cotton candy at the fair.

"Damn right," said the cop in a gruff voice.

After an evening of making a thirteen-year-old's dreams come true, watching her dance with her friends and every cop that was there, Lexi was wearing my too big suit jacket as she climbed back into the truck.

"How was your first dance, Squirt?" I asked, starting it and backing out of the parking place.

"So much fun." she said softly, staring out the window.

"What's on your mind?"

"Dad would've loved it," her tiny voice came to me in the dark cab, lit only by the dashboard.

She turned her head, her hair so much like her father's coming out of the updo her mom had put it in, smiling sadly at me.

Suddenly choked up at her soft statement, I reached over, patting her hand and giving it a gentle squeeze.

"He sure would've, sweetheart."

CHAPTER SEVEN
TREVOR

"You really think she's turned a corner?"

Becks' soft voice came to me from the driver's side of her SUV, leaning up to peer at me around Lucas.

I smiled reassuringly and nodded at her.

"We've been talking a lot more than we had been lately. She's letting me help her with things, and willing to ask for help when she needs it. She even had me over for dinner the other night."

It had been a couple weeks since I'd found Monica sitting in front of that nightstand in tears. I'd seen the handwriting on the envelope. Paul's messy scrawl had driven all of us nuts when he'd been alive. Monica was constantly misunderstanding telephone messages or notes he may write down instead of texting. He hated texting. I hadn't pushed to know what was in it. Just helped her to her feet and wrapped her in a huge hug. We'd finished emptying the room.

Her and the girls seemed lighter. They'd gone shopping that

night and Lacey had even texted me funny pictures of them in the store picking out decor and bed items. I had been shocked when Lacey had even thanked me for helping and trying to come around even more. Usually she was so hesitant to instigate communication in her teenage years that it knocked Mon and I sideways when she was nice to us.

Becks' eyes lit up and Lucas groaned.

"I know that look. It means you have an idea," he quipped.

Beck's small hand slapped his muscular arm.

"Shut up. I was just thinking Trev should start coming to our weekly dinners at Monica's!"

A warm feeling moved through me at the idea of it.

"I don't know, guys. That seems like a couple thing."

"Lucas and I weren't together when I started joining them for weekly dinners with Monica and Paul," argued Becks.

"Yeah. And just look how that turned out," her husband laughed.

"Would that be so bad?" asked Becks.

Both of us swung our gaze to the woman. Me wondering if I was that transparent about wanting my ex-wife again, Lucas in shock at her suggestion.

"What is with women and matchmaking? Dude, I'm sorry-" he began.

"It's fine." I said, winking at Becks. "I have to get on shift though. Thanks for dropping these by for me." I held up the cookies Lucas' wife and Natasha had made me. "The guys will appreciate these."

"Just make sure you get at least one before they're gone this time," she returned laughing.

Becks was apparently in some sort of baking kick. Lucas

chalked it up to the pregnancy and feeling more motherly than usual. They'd started telling people the last couple of days that she was expecting. I was happy for them. Monica had gloated that she knew before anyone else did after Lucas and the doctor.

I waved them off as I turned and looked at the firehouse. Working the night shift was typically quiet. Something felt off tonight though. I wasn't sure what it was. After being a firefighter for so long you start to develop a sixth sense about these things.

Brushing it off, I walked on in, greeting my coworkers and grabbing a cookie from the bag before placing it in the middle of the table. The men in this firehouse were like bloodhounds on the scent when free food was available. They'd be gone within minutes.

A couple hours later, nearing midnight, my phone went off.

Monica

> Would you want to come to our weekly dinner? Usually it's just the girls, Lucas, Becks, and Nat.

> Did Becks get a hold of you?

> LOL. Maybe. But I should've thought of it and asked before now. I feel bad. If you're as lonely as I can get, I know it can be rough. Unless it's different for men and you have tons of hot dates on your evenings off and weekends.

> There's no other woman in my life, Monica. Just you and the girls.

I raised an eyebrow, watching the three dots move across the screen like she was typing. They stopped and disappeared several times before her message finally came through.

> You could probably do better than your widowed ex-wife, Trev. LOL.

> I don't know. Seems like we already know each other well enough to skip the awkward phase of dating someone new.

Complete silence came over my screen. I really couldn't believe I'd gone there. It was quicker than I'd intended. I was just so weary of waiting and pining over her. The silence continued and I knew she was in her head.

> What are you doing anyway? The brats causing trouble?

> Nice deflection. No. Lacey went to bed a while ago and said she had a headache. I peeked in and she was under the covers completely. Head and all. So I didn't disturb her. Lexi conned me into letting her spend the night with Nat.

> You should get some rest then.

> Are you saying I need my beauty sleep?

> You're gorgeous. You just need to take care of yourself. Night.

> Night.

Well then. That had just happened. Shaking my bangs off of my forehead I sighed, scrubbing my hands over my face. She didn't seem completely freaked out or opposed. Just hesitant, and I could get that. I was hesitant in some ways to destroy the peace we had.

The fire house's alarm crashed through the building and

everything stopped. I went into work mode as the speaker burst to life with the alert on what had happened. Two car accident. Civilian on scene. No emergency personnel yet. Within seconds myself and the guys were in the truck, sirens blaring and speeding down the streets towards the location. My adrenaline was pumping. This was what I loved about my work. Every call. We'd get there and save lives. I never pictured any other alternative until the situation screamed we were too late.

Jumping out of the truck on my side, my jaw clenched taking in the scene. A truck was sideways on the road with an older gentleman sitting behind the wheel, shaking his head.

I overheard him.

"It was the darndest thing. The car just ran the stop sign and came out of nowhere. I was going sixty, I couldn't break in time-"

Walking up to the small sports car that was now on its passenger side, I hit my stomach, palms slapping the pavement to peer into the window.

Just to meet the green eyes of my petrified daughter, hanging upside down, staring at me with tears streaming down her face.

"Daddy?" her voice was small and shaking, breathless in her terror. My entire body was clenched, unprepared for this scenario. She was supposed to be home safe in her bed. *What the fuck?!*

"Don't move." I spoke brusquely, my voice calmer than I felt. "What hurts? What happened? Dammit. It's my daughter!" I yelled at my coworker who had stopped behind me. I met his wide-eyes and he moved, relaying the information.

I wouldn't be able to handle this as much of a professional and they would have to pick up whatever slack if I broke.

"I'm so sorry." Lacey was sobbing now.

"Hey. We're not talking about that right now, baby. We just

need to get you out of here."

My eyes moved past her taking in the unconscious form of the boy she was with.

"Have you all been drinking?" I asked briskly.

"No. I promise. I just wanted to hang out with him. I know I shouldn't have snuck out. Mom doesn't know-"

"I know your mother doesn't know." I replied. "She thinks you are home, safe in bed, with a headache. Where you should be. Give me a minute."

Standing and running my fingers through my hair, "FUCK!" I let out, in a quiet yell.

My coworkers got to work pulling out backboards and getting the two kids out of the car. Whoever-the-Fuck-He-Was looked to be about Lacey's age. Maybe older. I yanked my phone out of my pocket. I hated doing this. Things had calmed down. But her mother needed to know.

"Hello?" Monica's sleepy voice answered me, becoming more alert as she heard the background noises and sirens. "Trevor? What's going on?"

"I need you to stay calm, Monica." I said, somewhat sternly.

"Okay, you're scaring me." she whispered now.

"Lacey isn't in bed. She snuck out. I responded to a car accident and it's her and some boy. She seems fine, but the car tipped sideways. We're removing them from it now. I'll ride with her to the hospital. I'm calling Lucas to come get you. I don't want you driving."

"What? Oh my fucking God!"

I could hear her scrambling, breath rushing in pants.

"I'm going to-" she began.

"You're not driving. I'm calling Lucas. Get dressed. Be waiting." I was terse, barely holding it together myself. "I need you safe too. You're not driving. Please." I was begging.

"Okay. Just….tell him to hurry! Tell Lacey I love her and I'm coming-"

"I will, just get dressed. I have our girl, Mon."

Hanging up, I jumped up behind my daughter who was strapped immobile onto a backboard now. Dialing Lucas, I gripped her hand, staring down at her green eyes swimming in tears as I asked him to go get Monica and bring her to us.

CHAPTER EIGHT
MONICA

"Lacey Connor. C-O-N-N-O-R. She was in a car accident and I'm her mother-"

"Mon. Slow down." Lucas' brusque voice came from behind me as his hand rested heavily on my shoulder. I felt like I was coming undone all over again. I had been waiting on the street when Lucas had gotten to my house earlier and practically been screaming at him to drive faster the entire way to the hospital.

"Monica!" Trevor's voice echoed behind us and I spun around, searching him out frantically. Seeing him coming toward me across the room, I rushed to meet him halfway as his hands came up to my arms. Why was everyone holding me back? Didn't they sense the urgency?

"Mon." Trevor spoke again, drawing my panicked eyes up to his.

"Breathe," he instructed. "In through your nose and out through your mouth. Three times for me, sweetheart."

I obeyed mindlessly as his eyes bore into mine, watching me, and nodding encouragingly.

Everything in my body was so tightly wound, just the extra deep breaths were calming me slightly. Bringing me out of a panicked head space where I wasn't even thinking rationally.

"Where is she? Is she okay?" my voice wasn't one I recognized. Trembling and shaky. I couldn't lose another person I loved.

"She's fine. Banged up and scared as hell. They're taking her for some scans just to be safe. But she's okay. She's fine." he repeated, drawing me against his chest. I didn't even think. My arms wrapped around his waist tightly, pressing my face against his chest as I sobbed. I felt his large hand find the back of my head, holding me against him like I was precious, his other running up and down my back soothingly as he thanked Lucas for getting me here safely and informing him we'd call him with more information later.

This felt nice. Having someone to rely on and hold onto me when I was scared. I'd missed this. I was a social person. I had cut myself off too much the last year and a half. I continued taking deep breaths, smelling Trevor's spicy cologne. My hands and arms were warm under his firecoat and I could feel the muscles under his shirt. He'd bulked up since we were younger. Reluctantly I drew back and wiped my eyes.

"You good?" he asked, looking down at me worriedly. His hand came up cupping my face gently, his thumb sliding over my cheek, collecting some of my tears.

"I'm fine. I'm sorry I keep crying on you—"

"You never have to apologize for that." he interrupted.

"What fucking boy was she with?" I blurted out suddenly, without a filter. Lacey was a bit boy crazy and always had been.

But she'd never had a serious relationship, or even brought someone home to introduce us to go on a date. I was floored that she'd been so deceptive and snuck out of the house.

Trevor's eyes hardened, going into protective father mode.

"Some Jackson kid. He's apparently nineteen. She met him at the pool earlier this summer? Said they'd been texting and he'd wanted to drive around and talk. She's a mess, Mon. She knows she fucked up."

"Damn right she fucked up!" I exclaimed. "She's grounded! FOREVER!"

Trevor's eyebrow rose, his piercing glinting under the fluorescent lighting.

"Easy, tiger." he scoffed. "I'm just as livid. But the more we come down on her, the more she's going to act out, I think."

I huffed. "Since when did you become the rational one?"

He just shook his head and grabbed my arm to lead me down the hallway to our daughter's triage room in the emergency department. The nurses were just getting her settled back into the bed. Her eyes met mine and instantly filled with tears. She looked so small and scared in that hospital gown and I instantly started sobbing again myself.

"Mom! I'm so sorry. I know what I did was stupid and-"

"Shhhhh." I said, going over and drawing her into my arms.

"Lacey," I whispered, "You could've been killed."

I broke off, my voice cracking.

She cried harder.

"Who is this boy? You've never mentioned a Jackson? He doesn't even sound like he's in your usual group of friends. Nineteen?" I drew back staring at her.

She avoided my eyes, picking at her fingernails.

"Jackson Flinton." she said. "I met him at the pool a couple of weeks ago. He graduated when I was a freshman. I knew of him in school-"

"Flinton?" Trevor interrupted. Turning my head I stared at him. His eyes were narrowed on our daughter. "As in Richard Flinton's son?"

Now Trevor's voice was rising, almost like he was panicking. My own eyes narrowed on him in concern at what this meant, head turning back towards my daughter questioningly.

"Yes?" she answered. Seeming to not understand whatever had her father on edge.

"WHERE'S MY BOY!" came bellowed from the hallway, right before a large hand yanked the curtain back from the room entrance.

A huge lumbering man stood there, breathing heavily. Dark eyes, wild and oily shoulder-length brown hair hung limply around his shoulders. He was wearing a stained white tank top and ratty jeans that had seen better days. They sagged around his waist, the belt not doing its job. A beer belly stood out and his arms were covered in tattoos. Not the artwork Trevor, Lucas, and all the guys had. These looked like poorly hashed out random ideas that were permanent mistakes. He reeked of alcohol and cigarette smoke.

Lacey cowered behind me at the intrusion and my body instinctively moved in front of her.

The man's eyes swung over us before landing on Trevor standing at the foot of the hospital bed.

"Well, well, well. Fancy seeing you here, old friend." he smirked, the nurse that had been attempting to stop him from entering our room, wringing her hands nervously.

"Is it?" Trevor's voice was hard and cold. I'd never heard it like this.

"Considering it was your fucking kid that had my underage daughter out past curfew?" Trevor's voice was clipped, shaking in rage, and I stood suddenly feeling the urge to restrain him.

The man laughed rudely, crossing his arms.

"My boys got good taste. It's a small world, Connor. Think you could move on and do better than all of us and just leave everything behind?"

"What is going on?" I interrupted, moving in front of Trevor, holding both hands out like I could hold these giant men back from each other. There was a volatile tension in the room and I was feeling slightly nauseous. I didn't need this happening in front of my child either, even if she was almost a grown woman.

"Must be the missus." The man spoke condescendingly to me. "Introduce us, Connor. We're old friends. We go way back."

"We're not friends, Richard." snapped Trevor, stepping forward, his flat, muscled stomach pressing into my hand. "Never were."

"Okay." I said. "I think you should leave, Mr. Flinton." My voice was coming out stronger than I felt at the moment.

Looking at this man's hard eyes, I sensed a danger. All my nerves were on high alert and I could feel myself about to lose it again.

"I'll leave." Richard smirked again. "But, I'm sure we'll be seeing each other again soon."

He left, the room reeking of his odor, and Lacey spoke first.

"Who was that?" her voice was small and timid.

Trevor shrugged out of his fireman's coat angrily and threw it in the hospital chair.

"That was your new boyfriend's father." he said, running both hands through his hair. "And someone from my past that I never wanted to see again. Let alone have involved with you two. Dammit, Lacey!"

He began pacing, and my dread grew. I felt like I may be sick.

"Who is he?" I asked. "What's so bad about him? Trevor?" I was begging as he was avoiding eye contact.

Trevor finally stopped and stared at me.

"He was my drug dealer, Monica."

My stomach felt like it hit my feet and my head jerked back like I'd been physically hit.

"Are you on drugs?" I spun on my daughter.

Her eyes were huge, staring at us.

"What? No! I've never even met his parents and didn't know who they were?" she exclaimed.

I spun back to Trevor, believing her, seeing the shock on her face, knowing it couldn't be an act.

"Trevor? How bad is this?" I asked.

"Bad." he replied, staring at Lacey and me.

"Fucking horrible."

CHAPTER NINE
TREVOR

"She's asleep."

My head came up, staring at my ex-wife as she came into her living room. I had taken up residence on the couch, my mind racing, trying to think of any way to avoid further contact with this man, his family and mine.

Monica came over, sitting beside me, turned towards me.

"Trevor-" she began.

"Monica. I am sorry-" I said at the same time.

She jerked back, her brown eyes wide with surprise.

"Sorry? What are you sorry for?" she asked.

"I did this. I brought him into my life all those years ago, and now he's back and-"

"Trevor. Shut the fuck up."

I stilled, looking at her.

"This isn't your fault. This is a relatively small city. They went to school together for a year. I've even seen him at sporting events.

It's not your fault. You've been clean for over a decade." she shook her head at me.

I sighed, leaning forward, the leather on the couch rubbing against my fireman uniform pants roughly. I'd removed the suspenders to hang loosely at my sides and had a white fitted shirt on. I scrubbed my hands over my face.

"Fuck!" I cursed into my calloused hands.

I felt Monica's tiny hand meet my back, rubbing soothingly. *Damn.* That felt good.

"I don't know how, but I promise to keep him and his son away from you all." I said, sitting up straight again, leaning into her touch, rolling my neck on my shoulders.

Monica leaned in suddenly, wrapping her arms around me tightly. Without a thought I brought my arms around her again, drawing her against me. It just felt right. Like no time had passed between us at all. Her body still seemed to fit mine perfectly. She was everything to me still. She even still smelled the same.

She was curvier and softer though. I found my hands moving along her back again as she snuggled closer, and let out a little sigh.

Shit. This feels too good, flitted through my mind briefly, but I needed it. I'd hold onto her as long as she'd let me. I felt her head move back and she tilted her neck up to look at me.

"Thank you." she said softly.

I met her eyes, looking down at her. The only light in the room coming from a lamp by the front window casting a soft glow around the room. I reached up, brushing some hair off of her forehead, tucking it behind her ear. I saw her pulse jump in her neck when I made contact with her skin.

"For what?" I asked, my voice coming out gruffly.

"Everything you've done for me."

"I'd do anything for you. Always."

Her eyes were huge, staring at me. She licked her lips nervously and my eyes were drawn to her mouth. I didn't think about it. I just lowered my head and pressed my mouth gently against hers. Brushing mine over hers lightly. I felt her sharp intake of breath and stilled, gauging her reaction.

She sighed and her hands clenched my shirt, pulling me closer and pressing her lips firmer against mine. Sliding my hand up the side of her neck gently, I tipped her head further back with my thumb, sliding it under her chin. My other arm stayed firmly around her waist, drawing her closer to me, deepening the kiss.

Whatever she was willing to give, I was going to take. I'd waited years for this. For a second chance. I teased the seam of her lips with the tip of my tongue.

Testing.

Daring.

Their pillowy softness parted on a sigh and I was home. My tongue sliding against hers. It was like the years had never happened.

Kissing Monica felt like coming home.

The pieces of my heart felt like they found their matches and were settling back into place. She hesitantly brushed her tongue against mine and I groaned into her. Then we were lost. Trapped in a suddenly heated kiss where we felt like we couldn't drink each other in fast enough. Her hands were sliding up over my shoulders, clutching me to her, and I pressed her into the back of the sofa, I could feel her breasts pressing into the hardness of my chest.

I needed to keep my head. This couldn't go too fast and

scare her. Ruin things for both of us. Breaking the kiss, we both breathed heavily. I rested my forehead against hers, moving my thumb soothingly over her cheek as she gazed into my eyes.

Clearing her throat softly, she spoke, "Well, then. That's new."

I snorted softly.

"It's been a long time coming for me, Monica."

"Yeah?" she asked hesitantly.

"Always." I replied, seriously.

She visibly gulped, and I decided things had progressed enough for one evening. Sitting back I adjusted my painfully hard erection in my pants and ran a hand through my hair again.

"Wanna go on a date?" I blurted out.

Smooth, dumbass.

Monica's hands flew up, clasping over her mouth, and she fell back giggling.

"Trevor! Our daughter was just in a car accident, after sneaking out of the house and going joyriding with your old drug dealer's son, and you're asking me on a date?"

I laughed, staring up at the ceiling, before meeting her gaze again.

"Apparently, Mon." I said seriously.

She stopped and stared at me. Seeming to take me in, her eyes moving over my face consideringly.

"I've never stopped loving you, Mon. I respected you and Paul. I was happy for you all and knew you'd moved on to someone more deserving. But, I've always had feelings for you. Always will."

I'd laid it all out. Nothing held back now.

"If there's anything the last year and a half has taught us, it's that life is fleeting and we shouldn't sit around and wait on things." I continued, nervously, looking away, through the front window and out onto the quiet, dark street.

"Okay." she whispered.

My head jerked to the side, staring at her disbelievingly.

"Okay?" I asked.

She nodded.

"We can go on a date."

She spoke so quietly I wasn't sure I'd heard her correctly. I was in a little bit of shock that the evening had turned out like this after all the drama. I blinked at her.

"Trevor." she snapped her fingers in front of my face. "You asked me, you goof. Why are you acting so shocked?"

I shrugged.

"I just never thought you'd give me another chance after the way I fucked up." my throat felt tight. Like I was going to start crying at any minute.

Monica's eyes softened as she looked at me.

"Everyone deserves a second chance, Trevor." she whispered, clasping my big hand in her tiny one. "Everyone."

I gazed into her warm, brown eyes.

"I should probably get back to the firehouse and finish my shift. Call me if you all need anything. I'll stop by tomorrow morning and check on Lacey." I stood, grabbing Monica's hand to help her up off the couch.

"I will. I was so scared tonight. I'm so relieved she's okay."

I nodded as she trailed me to the door to lock it behind me.

"Never thought she'd be the type to sneak out of the house though."

Monic snorted.

"Well you are her father, Trevor."

"Watch it." I said, playfully. Grabbing her by the waistband of her leggings and bringing her against me roughly, she gasped. Before she could say anything I ducked my head and kissed her hard, nipping at her lower lip.

"I'll text you to set up that date." I said, drawing back and staring into her now glazed eyes as she nodded up at me.

Smirking, I turned and walked out the door to head back to work.

CHAPTER TEN
RICHARD

"I don't really give a fuck what you do or don't want you un-grateful piece of shit." I stood over my son, cowering in his hospital bed.

"Dad. She's literally just a friend though."

"I'm not asking you to marry the girl, Jackson. I'm asking you to get close to her. Draw her in. I can use this."

My son was eying me wearily. He had too much of his fuck-ing mother in him. Wherever the hell that whore had ran off to. Leaving me to raise this whelp on my own. He couldn't even live up to my expectations.

"Its either that or you drop out of that fucking fancy college and join the family business." I growled.

"Fancy school? You send me to community college." he snapped back at me.

"And you're lucky I'm doing it." I got in his face, hand on his chest roughly. I didn't give a fuck if he had broken ribs and a con-

. He thought he was too good for this life. It was paying for his fucking prissy boy education. He could start manning up. I couldn't think of anything better than getting revenge on the shit head that had gotten clean and ratted us all out.

"Fine." he finally gasped, grimacing in pain.

The door opened behind us as I backed away quickly, a nurse rushing in.

"Is everything okay? The monitors were going wild. Are you in pain, sweetheart?" she addressed my boy, not even looking at me.

"He's fine." I stated firmly. "Don't baby him, he's not a pussy."

The petite nurse glared at me now. Feisty this one.

"I'll get you some more pain medicine, hon. Perhaps visitors should go home for the night." She stared at me pointedly.

"I'll see you tomorrow." I directed at my son.

"Have a good night, gorgeous." I mimicked blowing a kiss to the nurse as she curled her lip in disgust.

Laughing, I walked out of the hospital room to return to my job on the streets.

CHAPTER ELEVEN
MONICA

"You kissed Trevor?" Becks was staring at me, sitting cross-legged on the couch in her living room. I'd brought Lacey with me after the evening we had. She was grounded for a few weeks. She, Lexi, and Nat were in Nat's bedroom doing teenage girl things.

Nat's two cats were prowling around on the floor, pushing a ball back and forth between them. Lucas had surprised her with them at Christmas time and they were adorable. The two brothers tumbled over each other, batting playfully as I watched.

"Shhhh." I hushed her, glancing up at the ceiling where the girls were.

"Sorry," she quieted. "This is a lot though."

She gripped her coffee mug full of hot tea and leaned forward, looking at me expectantly.

"How was it? Was it just kissing? Or did you-"

"Whoa!" I said, waving my hand. "Yes, we just kissed. Well,

twice. He gave me another one, before he left, that kind of took my breath away."

I placed my own mug of coffee down on the table between us and touched my lower lip absentmindedly, remembering his small nip he'd given me there. Becks' eyes lit up watching me.

"Oh, this is too good." she squealed, uncrossing her legs and kicking her feet.

Rolling my eyes, I picked up a cupcake that she'd made and bit into it to avoid talking.

"Mmmmm," I moaned. "Becks, these are amazing!" I exclaimed with a full mouth.

"Thanks." she waved me off. "Do you wanna sleep with him?"

I choked, coughing, and grabbing my coffee again to take a sip.

"Rebecca Marshall!" I sputtered.

"Oh, shut up. You were the same way with Lucas and I." she snorted. "I need details."

Quirking my eyebrow, I spoke, "Is everything okay in married life?"

"Yes. Lucas is just being weird. I'm four months along and everything is fine. I haven't even been sick. But he's never been with someone who's pregnant. He's so weird about it. He's scared he's going to hurt the baby."

I laughed out loud at that.

"Paul was the same way when I was pregnant with Lexi. Trevor didn't have that problem when I was pregnant with Lacey though." I tilted my head consideringly. "If anything it made him want me more. Not that Paul didn't want me. He just was creeped out there was a baby and convinced Lexi knew what we were doing. Weird because Trevor and I were younger. You'd think he would've been freaked out. Trevor, he didn't ever have any hangups when it came to sex."

Rebecca was leaning forward now, grinning.

"Oh really?" she questioned.

I shrugged.

"He was so much more street smart than me when we met. He was my first and he already knew his way around a woman's body. He is a take charge type of guy." I blushed.

Becks groaned and fell back on the couch.

"You'd think I'd be okay having gone thirteen years without sex and ever without good sex. Now that I've had really good sex though, I miss it. Lucas needs to snap out of it." she was whining.

Laughing, I nodded.

"You may have to take charge. Why don't I take Nat tonight and you can plan a surprise for Lucas when the boys are done? Something he can't turn down."

Trevor and Nick had met Lucas at his tattoo artist's shop today. Marcus and his co-worker were doing matching memorial tattoos on them for Paul. It meant a lot to me and warmed my heart. They still felt so passionately about his friendship. Lucas had gotten his done within days. Sprawled across his massive forearm, "I am my brother's keeper" with Paul's badge number.

Nick and Trevor had loved it and wanted them immediately. Today was the first day they'd all been able to go together.

"That may be a good idea," said Becks' staring at the ceiling consideringly. "What do you bet Lucas comes home with new ink even though he didn't have an appointment?" she asked.

Leaning back on my own seat, I smirked.

"I'm not taking that bet. Lucas can't go more than a month without some new tattoo. When are you going to break down and get one?"

Becks' shuddered. She absolutely hated needles and anything involving them. I didn't blame her, they weren't my favorite thing either.

"I'll get one when you do." she promised, looking over at me from where she laid on her back.

"Ok. So when pigs fly?" I joked, tossing a pillow over at my laughing friend.

"We could get friend's ones though. Small ones." she considered.

I nodded. We were often able to share easy, comfortable silences without talking. We just sipped our drinks for a bit, watching the quiet street in front of their home.

"Mom! Lacey just called me a brat!" shrieked Lexi from upstairs.

Groaning, I dropped my head onto the back of the couch.

"What has gotten into her?" I questioned. "They always fight, but this is extreme lately. And sneaking out last night?" I picked my head up looking at Becks.

She grimaced, shrugging.

"Lacey!" I yelled. "Downstairs now!"

Stomps followed, nearing the stairs, and thundering down them towards us.

I mouthed an apology to Becks and she just waved her hand, brushing me off.

"First of all" I looked at my surly oldest when she entered the room. "Apologize to your Aunt Becks for treating her home like that."

"Fine. Sorry." Lacey snapped, crossing her arms and avoiding eye contact. She stared at her flip-flop shod feet. I looked her over in her shorts and t-shirt and shook my head. Something was very off with my oldest. She'd always had a teenage attitude but wasn't ever outright defiant like this.

"It's okay, Lacey," said Becks, gently, standing and picking her mug up. "I'm just going to get some more decaf tea." She paused when she got near my daughter and leaned over whispering something to her before kissing the side of her head gently and moving on into the kitchen.

Lacey at least smiled at that and then looked over at me.

"What is going on, honey?" I asked, flabbergasted. "First sneaking out and the fighting with your sister is escalating now into name calling? You're moody and-"

"I'm fine." she interrupted.

"Lacey."

"Mom! I said I'm fine! I'm just tired and sore. I'm stressed about my senior year." she said, looking at me.

I sighed, staring at her.

"You know your dad and I love you. We're always here for you to talk to. You don't have to hold all of this in. You can talk to me about anything. Hell. Talk to Becks if you don't want to talk to your mom, Lacey. Just promise me you won't keep on like this." I begged. "I can't lose you too."

"You're not going to lose me, Mom. God." she rolled her eyes and made her way over, sitting beside me.

"Well, I sure miss my sweeter moments with you." I joked, wrapping an arm around her and drawing her close.

"I'm almost a grown-up." she grumbled.

"You'll always be my baby though." I whispered, squeezing her.

"Awww. Look at you two." said Becks from the entryway into

the kitchen. "Did you all make up?"

Lacey laughed, sitting up and pulling away from me. I rubbed my chest over my heart absently.

I hadn't been lying when I said I was scared I was going to lose her. She was growing up too fast. Paul and she had been so close even though he was just her step-dad. He could get her to cut up and laugh. She'd talked to him about things a lot more than me. We were just too much alike.

Becks smiled at me, knowingly, taking her spot on her couch again.

"Can I babysit when the baby comes?" asked Lacey suddenly.

I jerked my head in surprise and Becks looked shocked too. We had to practically beg her to watch Nat and Lexi when we wanted her to.

Becks nodded. "That's definitely something we can talk about Lacey."

Lacey smiled at her and stood up.

"Thanks, Aunt Becks. I'm sorry again. I'm going back up-stairs."

We watched her leave the room and I shook my head.

"Talk about a roller coaster of moods." I mumbled.

Becks laughed. "She's at a confusing time in her life."

"Who's gonna tell her it never gets better?" I joked.

Becks just lifted her mug of tea in a toast to the accurateness of my statement.

CHAPTER TWELVE

TREVOR

Tilting my review mirror down I checked my hair again. Sitting in my red pickup truck outside of Monica's house felt different this time. I felt like I was sixteen again, picking her up for our first ever date. I'd been nervous then too. Imagining what her parents would be like, do, or say. I'd grown up with two miserable excuses for parents. Constantly cheating on one another, fighting, using each other as punching bags. Using their only child as a punching bag, I'd been nervous as hell to walk into that house then. But her parents had been nothing but welcoming and understanding. They'd ended up saving me in a way.

They gave me the first normalcy I'd ever had. The first stability. I felt like I'd thrown it all back in their face after I'd gone down my own drug-addled path and left Monica and Lacey. But they'd welcomed me back with open arms when I'd gotten my shit together.

I was nervous as hell and her parents weren't even there this time to greet me. We were grown adults. We'd spoken to the girls about everything. They were surprisingly okay with it all. Lexi was more nervous than Lacey, understandably. I was pretty sure she felt like I was going to try to replace Paul in some way.

That was never my intention and never would be. His memory would stay alive in all of us. I rubbed at my healing tattoo absentmindedly before opening my truck door and climbing down. The memorial piece I'd gotten for Paul was an amazing work of art. Lucas had voiced his idea to his tattooist, Marcus, and he'd brought the vision to life. Nick and I had gotten them together last week while Lucas talked and joked around visiting with us in the shop.

I pressed the doorbell and stuck my free hand in my jean pocket nervously. I'd tried to keep it casual but looked nicer than I usually did. I preferred my sweatpants and casual t-shirts. The jeans and tight fighting polo were not my usual attire.

The door swung open and my daughter stood smirking at me. She looked so much like me sometimes it was breathtaking.

"Hey, beautiful." I said, stepping in and giving her a hug. She scoffed, pushing me away.

"Mom's still finishing getting ready." She led me into the living room where Lexi was sitting with a movie paused. She smiled at me hesitantly. Crouching down in front of her, I handed her a small bundle of wildflowers I'd bought at the flower shop in town.

"Here you go, beautiful. Thanks for letting me take your mom out." I grinned at her.

She smiled more openly and her eyes lit up at the bouquet.

"Thanks, Trevor!" she exclaimed.

"You're welcome. I want you to know, both of you, that I'm not stepping in to replace anyone. That's never going to be my intention. I loved your dad too. He was like a brother to me." my voice grew tight, as I stared into Lexi's eyes, willing her to believe me.

She nodded, red hair falling into her face, but not before I saw some tears in her eyes.

I sighed and stood, turning and presenting another small wildflower bouquet to my oldest.

"Dad!" she exclaimed, rolling her eyes. But she took it and smiled all the same.

"Almost out of solitary confinement?" I asked her, crossing my arms, fumbling with the much larger bouquet I'd bought their mother.

"Just a few more days." Lacey returned, smiling up at me.

"Your mother was too easy on you. She talked me down from a month long grounding, you know." I said, staring at her.

"I know." her voice was meek, and she looked at her bare feet.

"We just love you, Lacey. We want the best for you. Don't screw it up like I did. You know I've been there. You know what it did."

She nodded, still avoiding eye contact.

"You're not still texting that Jackson kid anymore are you-"

"Trevor!"

I spun around, staring at Monica as she came down the stairs. All conversation with my oldest was forgotten at that moment. Wearing sandal flats and a flowy, summer dress, Monica looked stunning. She'd put on some light make-up and left her brown hair down around her shoulders. Her eyes were sparkling behind her glasses.

"Damn, you look hot." I blurted out.

"EW!" Both girls exclaimed behind us as Monica threw her

head back and laughed.

I blushed. *Fucking blushed for God's sakes.* Thrusting the huge bouquet of wildflowers out toward Monica, I just smirked at her.

"These are beautiful. Thank you, Trev." she said softly. Her eyes took in the scene, seeing the girls' smaller bouquets.

"What do you say we go in the kitchen and I get some vases for our flowers?" she said, "You all can put them in your rooms."

Both girls followed her and I followed them, enjoying watching them together, their unity.

The usual spats took place, Lexi wanting the purple vase that her older sister did. I watched my oldest's face turn red. Her anger far surpassed what the situation called for. I was worried about her. She reminded me so much of myself at that age. If it hadn't been for Monica, I'd have gone off the deep end far sooner than I had.

"Lacey," I said, softly, but sternly, As I cut off what was sure to be some scathing remark.

She sighed heavily.

"Fine, take the purple vase." she plopped her own bouquet in a blue one and stalked up the stairs to her bedroom, slamming the door.

Monica cringed as I watched her and shook her head, meeting my eyes.

The doorbell rang again and Lexi went to answer it, carrying her flowers.

"I don't know what's gotten into her. She's acting out so much more lately." she said.

We heard Lexi greeting Becks, Lucas, and Nat before the younger girls' footsteps thundered up the stairs to Lexi's room.

Lucas and Becks walked into the kitchen.

"Thank you guys for coming over to watch the girls. I really didn't want to leave Lexi alone with Lacey while she's grounded and acting out so much."

Becks shook her head.

"It's not a problem." said Lucas, grabbing my hand to pull me in for a quick, chest-bump kind of hug. "You know we love spending time with those girls."

"Plus it gets you two out on a date." Becks teased, grinning.

"Yes it does. And, we need to go. Our reservations are in twenty minutes at Mellandro's." I said, looking at the time on my phone.

"Mellandro's?" said Monica. "Trevor, that's too much. I'd have been fine with a burger-"

"Shut up and let the man spoil you, woman!" exclaimed Becks.

Monica glared at her best friend as Lucas laughed.

"Shoo, you two. Get out of here. There's no curfew. GO!" Becks started corralling us to the front door.

"Don't do anything I wouldn't do, kids." said Lucas, laughing at his wife's antics.

"Call me if you need anything. Seriously, Becks. Lacey is being horrible." said Monica as we stood on the front porch.

"We'll be fine! GO!" Becks said, swinging the door closed.

"Well then." I said, grabbing Monica's hand and leading her to the passenger side of the truck. "That's that."

I opened the door and, before she could protest, grabbed her and lifted her up so she didn't have to worry about her dress.

She looked at me with huge eyes.

"Trevor, I'm too heavy for you to be doing that." she blushed, turning and buckling up.

"The hell." I replied. "I've carried grown men out of burning buildings, woman. I can toss you around any time you want."

She looked at me, her eyes slightly darker now, as she took me in.

"You have filled out quite a bit since we were in our twenties." she spoke, her voice slightly huskier.

"You have no idea." I smirked, shutting the door.

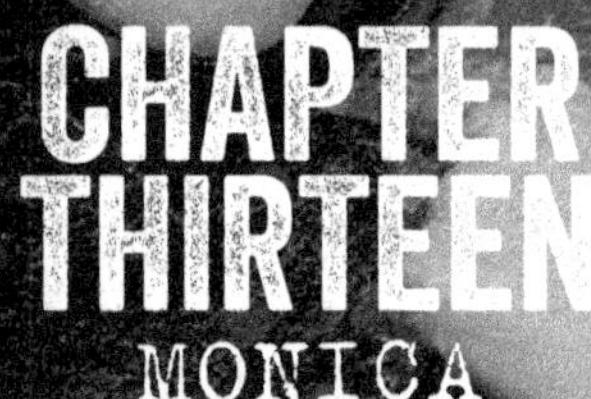

CHAPTER THIRTEEN
MONICA

Laughing, I threw my ice-cream cup in the trash can alongside Trevor's. We'd had a wonderful meal at my favorite restaurant and he'd suggested dessert from the local ice cream shop with a walk in the park. Conversation had been easy and it seemed like we had picked up right where we'd left things before they'd gone so badly in our relationship.

Trevor reached over, lacing his fingers through mine like it was second nature and I felt like a thousand butterflies took flight in my stomach. This was slightly ridiculous. I was a grown woman. Divorced, two kids, widowed, and I was getting butterflies on a date with my ex-husband and father of one of my children. He looked amazing tonight. His shaggy blonde hair he always left longer in the front getting in his eyes. He always had to shake it out of them in a move that had melted me since high school.

Tight, acid-washed jeans and a polo that fit him like a second skin. I'd had trouble keeping my eyes off him all night long. He looked like he'd filled out, gotten muscular, leaner with age. While I'd gotten softer after having a couple of babies and was suddenly unsure of my body.

I'd only been with two men in my life. One when I was still young and fitter and the other my husband of fourteen years.

Even though Trevor used to know me and my body, I was terrified he wouldn't like how I'd changed.

"What's going through that gorgeous head of yours, Mon?" asked Trevor, yanking me closer to him and throwing his arm around my shoulder.

"Just how it's unfair men age so gracefully and women don't." I snorted in return, looking up at him.

He quirked a brow, his eyebrow ring catching my eye momentarily. Even that was hot. Piercing and tattoos. I was a sucker for both.

"You saying you think I'm hot?" he laughed, obviously joking.

"Basically. And way outa my league at this point in our lives." I joked.

"Whoa," he said, pulling me to a gentle stop. "You are anywhere but out of my league, Monica." he looked down at me, the stars in the sky twinkling overhead.

I blushed.

"What I see is a young girl I fell in love with in high school, that has matured into a fucking gorgeous woman. Who has an amazing body, that has grown and brought life to two beautiful little girls. That body has nurtured them and sustained them. If you don't think that turns me on, you're crazy." he said, his voice deeper now, resting his hands on my hips.

They felt like scorching heat through my lightweight dress. I was hyper aware of how close he was to me, towering over me. If I took a deep enough breath, my chest would brush against his. I found myself swaying closer to him, hands resting softly against his chest. *God, these muscles.* I felt like a sixteen-year-old again. I wanted him to kiss me, but didn't know how to ask for it. The feel of his mouth on mine a week ago had awoken something in me I thought had died with Paul.

His finger trailed down my jawline, sliding under my chin and tilting my head up more. His green eyes were darker, more mossy, heated, and made my entire body warm.

"Ask for it." he spoke, his voice low and practically a growl.

I shivered in response, playing coy.

"For what?" I said, my voice unintentionally husky. I blinked up at him, shocked at the reaction my body had to him.

Two of his fingers clasped my chin.

"For what your eyes are fucking begging me for, Monica." he brought his face down low, nose barely brushing against mine. His breath was hot against my face, and I was gasping, breathing back into him.

"Kiss me." I stated, more breathy than I'd intended.

He growled and it rumbled low in his chest, his hand moving up, threading through the hair at the nape of my neck and clenching to tilt my head back more. His other muscled arm banded around my waist, drawing me tight against him, creating sparks everywhere our bodies touched.

Then his lips were on mine.

He commanded the kiss and my body. Nothing had changed there. He was just a man instead of a boy now. Mouth slanting over mine, my lips parted on a soft moan as his tongue took possession of my mouth. Stroking my own against his, he groaned and clenched his hand tighter in my hair. I felt like my body was coming awake at that bite of pain mixed with the pleasure he was giving me in this kiss. My hands gripped his shirt, pulling him further against me and arching into him.

I didn't care we were in the middle of the city park and anyone could walk up on us. I wanted this. The feeling of being out of control. Not having to worry about or fix anything. Losing myself in someone stronger made me feel safe. I moved my hands up around his neck, kissing him back just as hungrily. I drug my nails along the sides of his neck gently, remembering even all these years later that it drove him nuts.

"Fuck," he muttered, against my lips. We were both panting, breathless, breathing in each other's oxygen.

"Fuck it." he said, pushing me back against the light pole on the path we were on. He wasn't one to push us into the shadows. He didn't care who saw us. He was daring someone to walk up on us. It just drove me higher, knowing he didn't care. He wanted to be seen with me.

"You taste amazing." he growled against my ear, still gripping my head, holding it motionless. He rocked his hips against me, his denim covered hips coming to rest in the softer cradle of mine. It brought a friction against the cleft of my thighs that made me moan softly.

He nipped at my ear lobe with his teeth, sucking the hurt away gently.

"How wet are you for me?" he asked, his breath hot and moist against my ear.

I blushed. I'd forgotten how vocal he'd always been, and closed my eyes, embarrassed suddenly at my body's response to him.

He pulled my hair gently.

"Look at me. Now." he commanded, pulling back.

I opened my eyes, staring into his, lost.

"How wet are you for me?" he repeated.

"Soaked." I whispered, breathless.

He growled again, ducking his head and kissing along my neck, before releasing me and pulling back. I took pleasure in the fact he had to adjust himself in his pants with a groan. I stayed, leaning against the pole, gathering my wits. Panting, watching as he brushed both hands through his hair, before he looked at me. His eyes raked over my body taking me in, at how he'd caused me to come apart so quickly disheveled.

"Why'd you stop?" I asked, suddenly bold again.

He gave me a somewhat cocky grin.

"Because you and I both know when I finally get inside you, you're going to fucking scream." he moved into my space again, towering over me, overwhelming me. "You're going to beg, whimper, and moan, and come for me multiple times before I'm done with you." he added, causing my breathing to pick up again. "And a public park isn't the place for that. At least not for the first time." he said.

"Jesus, Trevor. Your mouth." I said, covering my face with my hands.

"Monica, you have no idea. No fucking clue." he said, grabbing my hand and continuing our walk, like he hadn't just shaken my entire world off its foundation.

Dating Monica again was refreshing. We'd settled into a comfortable pattern of weekly dinners with friends, hanging out with the girls, and dating. To be honest I was about to crawl out of my skin wanting her. I was trying to be respectful of the newness of our second chance relationship, but I could only take so many cold showers.

"Man, you are in your head today." Nick's voice startled me out of my thought process as I looked over to meet his gaze. The bar was packed tonight, hard to comfortably walk through and the wait staff was buzzing back and forth looking a little harried.

"Trouble with Mon?" This time my eyes found Lucas' across the booth. We'd been trying to get together for more guys' nights since Paul had passed. Making more time for friendships seemed important.

"Seriously? We're gonna sit here and talk about relationships?" I quirked a brow, tilting my water bottle up to take a long drink.

"You're avoiding the question." Stated Nick from his seat beside me, tilting his head. "Spill."

"Not before Lucas comes clean about his hangup regarding sleeping with his pregnant wife." I returned.

Nick's jaw dropped as Lucas sputtered, choking on the drink he'd just taken.

I threw my head back and laughed loud enough it turned a few heads despite the loud music.

"Women talk, and Monica told me all about it. Becks is seriously frustrated from what it sounds like. What's the hangup?" I asked, twirling the water bottle absentmindedly between my hands as I looked at my friend.

"I don't have a hangup" argued Lucas defensively. "I just don't want to….hurt anything." He trailed off.

Nick barked a laugh and I drug a hand over my face shaking my head.

"Lucas. Unless you're built unlike any man I've ever met, it's not going to hurt anything. If anything, women are so much more responsive when they're pregnant. Monica was practically feral when she was expecting Lacey."

Lucas looked like his eyes were about to bug out of his head. Nick looked like he was enjoying himself watching us gab at each other like old women.

"Suck it up and get back in the saddle. Do us all a favor. You've been grumpy as fuck the last five months. I can't imagine how you'll be in another four."

"We've done stuff!" He snapped, affronted. "Jesus. How much do these women talk?"

"Enough to know you're treating Becks like she's made of glass. It is not working in your favor in the bedroom, brother." I elbowed Nick as he snorted beside me.

"Oh, that's rich. Coming from someone who hasn't sealed the deal with someone he's had eyes on for over a decade and Mr. I-don't-do-relationships over here." He volleyed.

Nick threw his hands up.

"I want no part of this. I'm happy as I am. I have a need, I find an outlet and that's it. I'm too old for this shit." He scoffed.

Lucas and I stared at our friend.

"I thought the same thing not too long ago." said Lucas, throwing a balled up straw wrapper at Nick.

"It's a little different when you've got specific tastes," Nick's voice was quieter, less sure, as he checked his phone to avoid the conversation suddenly.

Lucas looked at me pointedly, raising his eyebrows and I shook my head at him to drop it.

Nick had always been a bit of a closed book. He'd never even let Paul get him set up when he'd been living and he and Monica had been known as the group's matchmakers.

All we knew was that Nick had always been single and never even had a date with a woman that we knew of. If he took women home for the night, we never heard about it, and neither did anyone else.

I shrugged, deciding to focus on one friend for the evening.

"I'm just waiting to make sure Monica's sure." I finally said, breaking the awkward silence.

"There's a lot of history there." Lucas agreed. "But according to Becks, Monica is getting frustrated herself." He smirked, lifting his own drink. "Monica talks too." He tapped his glass of bourbon against my water bottle, cockily.

Monica was frustrated?

I blew out a breath, running a hand through my hair, as Lucas and Nick started talking about something down at the police station. Maybe I was being too careful and it was time to just go for it. Every time things had gotten heated the last month and I'd pulled back she had seemed increasingly snippy with me.

I really had been trying to be considerate. Maybe I'd do us both a favor and quit stopping us. I'd been waiting for some major signal from her. Some blatant "pass go" sign. Monica had never been that way though.

"You and Becks have plans for Friday?" I asked, not even aware of what part of their conversation I'd interrupted.

Lucas and Nick both stared at me.

"I think we're free?" Lucas responded. "Becks has been tired earlier in the evenings. We just keep it chill at home. What's up?"

"Think you all could let the girls have a sleepover?"

Lucas smirked as Nick finished his beer.

"I think we can make that work."

"Mon and I will have to return the favor." I nodded.

Nick started laughing.

"Never imagined you all would be at the point in your lives you needed to find childcare to hook up." He teased, good-naturedly.

Lucas laughed and picked up their conversation from before I'd interrupted.

Yeah. Childcare was going to be necessary for what I had planned for Monica.

I smiled and finished my water.

"So, you're still talking to the daughter like I told you to?

My eyes jerked up to meet my son's across the dimly lit folding table in the trailer where we lived.

Using a razor I worked on cutting more cocaine into portions on the mirror I had laid out. I smirked, lining up the scale and mini bags to portion everything out. Jackson was squirming, clearly uncomfortable.

Pussy.

"Yes. But I'm not getting anywhere. She keeps saying she doesn't feel that way about me. I can't keep doing this. Her mom hangs out with cops. Her stepdad used to be a cop."

"Her fucking stepdad got what was coming to him. Should have taken out that fucking Marshall and his old lady too."

I'd sold to one of their victims, Larry, while he'd been local. He'd been one of my best customers and I was still pissed at the loss of a client.

Jackson quieted and I stared up at him.

"Unless you're ready to work these streets you'll keep doing what I fucking tell you. You know the consequences if you don't."

Jackson glared at me. Fucking brat thought he was better than this. Better than us. I don't know why I hadn't gotten rid of him long before now.

"I just need to hear about the bitches' father. The comings and goings. Keep trying. Or maybe I send one of the other guys to find her when she's alone? Do the job for you?" I shook a baggie, closing it, before leaning over the table and glaring up at him.

"I bet Chuck or Mike would like a job. A young thing like that-"

"I've got this!" He practically shouted. "Don't get them involved."

Too easy.

"Keep in line then." I grunted, watching him nod and slam out of the trailer.

I cut another line with shaky hands and bent to snort it myself.

Ahh. Clarity.

CHAPTER SIXTEEN
MONICA

Here I was. A grown woman, avoiding knocking on the apartment door in front of me.

I felt like my stomach was going to do a complete somersault inside of me at the prospect of a dinner and movie night at my boyfriend's apartment. A night free of the kids. Boyfriend? Was that too base of a term for what we were? Ex-spouse? How many people dated their ex-spouses?

I snorted softly at myself, glancing down at my baggy t-shirt and leggings. Maybe I should've dressed up? I had left my hair down. I touched my brunette strands where they stopped just past my shoulder nervously.

It's not like it would be our first time together if we had sex tonight. But, it had been over fifteen years since we'd been together sexually. I'd been married for fourteen of those. Happily. I'd had an entire baby since then. I'd put on fifteen or twenty pounds too.

I looked up at the ceiling, drawing on my usual courage,

pushing my glasses up.

"Mon?"

I jolted, looking back at the now open door where Trevor stood, blonde hair falling into his eyes slightly, relieved to see him in his usual gray sweatpants and a black tank top. He rested one hand on the upper door frame, leaning towards me slightly. The position showed off his muscles and tattoos gloriously.

Holy hell.

"Are you having a stroke?" he asked, jokingly. "You've been standing out here for fifteen minutes.

"Shut up." I said, snapping out of it and walking past him and into the apartment with more bravado than I currently felt. I heard the door shut and the click of the lock behind me. Drawing in a deep breath, I dropped my tote bag onto the recliner, and turned to face him.

"What on earth smells this amazing?" I asked, staring at him. "Did you order out?"

"No. I cooked," he returned, walking into the kitchen and checking a couple of pots on the stove.

I stared at his back, dumbfounded.

"You cooked?" I repeated. "And the apartment building isn't on fire?"

He laughed while I giggled.

The Trevor I'd known when we were dating, and married, hadn't been able to fix a frozen pizza without something going wrong.

"Yep," he let the sound of the "p" pop as he turned to let his eyes run over my body casually. "One of the many things I learned to do in rehab and on fire shifts," he said. "Plus I wanted to learn to cook for when I had Lacey." he shrugged, crossing his arms.

My stomach did a little swoosh and I felt myself melting a little bit. Something about men and their children did that to me.

I walked over to stand beside him, lifting the lid curiously, as he watched me with a small smile.

"Herbed chicken and rice pilaf?" I exclaimed. "Are you trying to feed me all of my favorite things?" I laughed, looking up at him.

His green eyes softened as they met mine.

"I want to do all your favorite things, always," he answered smoothly.

My cheeks heated with a blush as I looked down, replacing the lid carefully.

"So, what movie are we going to watch?" I was very good at deflecting when things were getting serious. It didn't help that I was thrown off. I'd expected take-out pizza later. Old Trevor would've had me up against the door before anything else had happened. I felt like I would've been less nervous if he'd just done that and we'd gotten it out of the way.

"I figured we could watch a comedy. Maybe? Or whatever you want if you have a girly movie you want to see?" he said, turning to start plating the food. He added a roll to both plates.

"Can you grab the rest of those in the bread basket?" He asked, walking towards his small kitchen table.

He really had a movie planned? Where was Trevor and what had this man done with him?

I stared at the bread basket filled with rolls in front of me and something inside of me snapped.

Before my brain could register what my body was doing I picked up a roll, turned, and threw it at the back of his pretty blonde head.

I covered my mouth as the roll made contact and pressed back against the counter. That was the most immature thing I'd done in ages. I had to blame the nerves.

His body stopped right by the kitchen table and he set the plates down slowly at the two settings he'd had ready. He turned around, pierced eyebrow cocked.

"Did you just throw a fucking dinner roll at me?"

I shrugged, trying my damndest not to start nervously giggling. I was definitely losing my mind.

"What the fuck, Mon?" he questioned.

"I don't know. I'm nervous as hell," I began "This is all new to me. You cooked dinner. You set the table. You're being a gentleman. The old Trevor would've just pushed me up against the door after he'd closed it and gotten the whole sex thing out of the way." I blurted out.

He crossed his arms, staring at me.

"Sorry?" I squeaked, even more nervous now.

Crossing the room towards me in long, steady strides, he crowded into my space. My back hit the hard edge of the countertop as I craned my neck back to look up at him.

"The Trevor you knew really, really well was a teenager and in his early twenties and fucked in the head." he said, bringing his hand up to rest on my chest at the base of my throat gently. My pulse was pounding and my breath was coming in soft pants.

"I'm thirty-eight years old now," he continued, his eyes moving down my body again like he owned it. "I still have the instinct to say fuck the dinner and bend you over this counter and fuck my claim into you." he leaned down, his breath hot and wet against my ear as I gasped, feeling his hard body press against my softer one.

"But I've waited a long fucking time for this and its not going to be some quick fuck against a door. I found that I like to savor and appreciate things now." He trailed his nose down my throat, sliding his hand up to squeeze my neck gently.

"I'm going to savor my dinner and then I'm going to savor you " he finished, standing up straight again. I watched him walk back to the table and stand behind a chair.

"Get your ass over here and sit down, Monica." he said, waiting to push the chair in.

Okay then, I thought to myself, walking over and doing what he said in a daze. He pushed me in gently, before moving my hair off my shoulder. Leaning down and kissing the side of my neck softly, causing me to close my eyes at the contact. When he took the seat across from me he smirked.

"Thank you. It looks amazing." I said, my voice cracking slightly with the underlying tension in the room.

"Fucking breathe, Mon" he laughed, pouring me some wine from the bottle he had on ice at the table.

"You make it hard to breathe," I blurted out, picking up my glass and taking a healthy drink.

Trevor's eyes darkened, across from me.

"You think you're having trouble breathing now?" he questioned, "Just wait until later."

He looked down, picking up his silverware and beginning his meal, while I just gaped at him.

How could this man just say and do the things he did and return to normal things like that?

Jesus.

"Eat, Mon." he said, breaking into my thoughts again. "You're going to need the energy."

So I ate.

Dinner was amazing and as we cleaned up the dishes together a little later, I could acknowledge that he'd set me at ease with the conversation. It felt very domestic to be helping each other with such a household chore. He was washing and I was drying while he told me where to put things.

I'd missed doing this with someone. Paul and I had liked doing this, sending the girl's to their room for homework every night. We'd enjoyed flirting with each other and talking about our days. It wasn't the exact same, but it was filling something inside my heart I was missing horribly.

"Where'd you go, beautiful?" asked Trevor, finishing rinsing the sink after cleaning it.

"Just enjoying doing this with you. Having someone to do this with." I said softly, fixated on hanging the towel perfectly to dry.

I could feel his eyes on me again and knew he could tell what I meant. His footsteps came up beside me as he drew me into a hug, holding onto me tight.

"You don't have to do that," he said softly.

"Hmm?"

"Avoid saying his name around me," he said. "My love for you is stronger than being jealous of something amazing you had with someone who took such good care of you and our girl." he said, rubbing my back.

My eyes teared up.

"Love?" I said, scoffing slightly. Wasn't it too soon for those words?

"I never stopped loving you. I'll always love you." he tilted my head back now to make eye contact.

Maybe it wasn't too soon. With our history, this was different territory. This man had held a candle for me for years. As his lips met mine gently, the last of my nerves ceased to exist.

CHAPTER SEVENTEEN

TREVOR

The tone of the evening kept changing. Nerves and sexual tension were running rampant between us. As my lips grazed over Monica's I sensed a change come over her. She went from emotional, lost in her memories, to present with me. She sighed, parting her lips, opening for me and I couldn't hold back any longer.

My tongue delved into her mouth, stroking, kissing her deep and hard as my body pushed her back against the counter again. She made a small whimper into my mouth and all my resolve snapped. I broke the kiss, panting, and staring down into her dazed eyes.

"You're gonna have to tell me now that this is okay." I breathed out, voice lower than normal, gravely. "I've gotten more patient but I still have my thresholds." I spoke, practically growling.

She nodded, trying to pull me down to her again.

"Words," is all I replied, hand coming up to her throat, holding her still gently.

"I want this," she whispered, breathless, "I want you."

That's all I needed to fucking hear.

Leaning down I took her mouth again, strong and fast. My hand left her throat, moving down to grab the back of her thighs and lift her onto the counter. She gasped and moved back to try to speak but I wasn't having it. I leaned her back, her head knocking into the cabinet, biting her lower lip then sucking it into my mouth. I broke off, backing up slightly.

"Take your shirt and bra off." I said, reaching behind my shoulder and pulling my own tank top off. Her eyes were like dark smoldering heat staring at me.

"Guess you're still bossy and controlling in the bedroom." she smarted off, lifting her shirt over her head. She was wearing a purple lace bralette underneath and I had to fight myself from lunging across to her again and ripping it off her body.

"Don't be a brat," I warned, "Or I'll make you beg for it."

Her eyes widened, chest heaving with her breaths.

"I haven't changed that much." I smiled at her.

She reached behind her unclasping the scrap of lace and let it fall. I groaned taking her in. She was clearly shy about how her body had changed but she was all woman now. The softness around her stomach, her heavier breasts, and her stretch marks turned me on. I was rock hard to the point of pain as I stared at her, barely able to restrain myself.

"Trevor," she begged softly, almost a whine.

"Tell me what you want."

"You."

"Details."

Her cheeks pinkend and her tongue darted out to lick her

lips nervously. She'd obviously forgotten how I could be and it was driving me on to bring this anticipation out in her again.

"I want your hands on me."

I stepped forward, running my hands down her arms, laughing darkly as she blew out a breath in exasperation.

Her smaller hands gripped my wrists, yanking my hands up to cover her breasts. I groaned at the contact, feeling her nipples harden against my palms. I squeezed, massaging them as her head fell back against the cabinet again.

"So responsive." I growled, leaning down and licking her right nipple softly before sucking it into my mouth. My right hand's thumb found her left breast's nipple flicking it softly.

"Trevor, please," she moaned.

"I told you I was going to savor you." I said, nipping at her hardened peak, breath hot against her breast.

"I don't want to be savored." she spoke, voice sure. "I need you inside me. Now."

I stood, looking down at her.

"Well, who am I to deny the woman I love what she needs?" I yanked her off the counter, spinning her around. My hands found the waistband of her leggings, yanking them down to reveal the matching purple underwear. There was no time to really enjoy the view. I could see her soaking them.

"Should I just move your panties to the side and fuck you with them on?" I whispered, arching over her, bending her to lay flat against the counter for me.

She whimpered softly and nodded, wiggling her ass back into me as I ground my hardness against her.

I lowered my sweatpants kicking them across the room as I stepped forward and kicked her feet further apart, her leggings still around her ankles.

"You look so beautiful, bent over my kitchen counter, trembling and soaking those purple panties." I praised, watching her, gripping the base of my hardened length before stroking myself.

"Trevor. Inside me. Now." she demanded.

I smirked. Coming up closer behind her again, I moved the lace to the side, revealing her bare and wet for me.

"Fuck, Monica," I growled, losing control. I rubbed the pierced tip of my cock against her folds, letting the ring hit her clit as she stiffened under me.

"Trevor?" she questioned "What is that?" she peeked back over her shoulder.

I raised my eyebrows, "Oh, just another piercing I got." I slid the tip down to her entrance, pressing teasingly to let her feel it.

Groaning, she backed up against me, taking about an inch in before I reached down, my large hand on the base of her spine, stopping her movement. I slid further into her heat, feeling her gripping me, trying to keep me inside as I let myself slide back out again, teasingly.

"Trevor!" she exclaimed, practically growling herself now.

"What, baby?" I asked innocently, running both of my hands up her back, soothing.

"Fuck me, now." she ordered, all shyness evaporating.

"There she is." I said, gripping her hips and thrusting my entire length inside her. We both groaned as my pelvis met her body. I was seated deep inside her, her wetness surrounding me, as I gritted my teeth, trying to keep still for a minute.

"Oh my God." she breathed, arching and adjusting to the feel of me inside of her. I laid my body over hers, curving around her, letting my hands trail down her arms to hers, lacing our fingers together.

"You good?" I asked, kissing the back of her neck as she nodded. I released one of her hands bringing my hand up to grip the base of her throat, pulling out and thrusting deep again as she moaned.

"You're with me?" I asked, one more time, just to be sure.

"Yes, Trev, please."

Then I was lost, flexing my hips and thrusting into her. She widened her legs slightly, trying to keep her footing as my hand tightened on her throat. Her fingers still interlaced with mine were gripping the counter as I moved in and out of her quickly. The wet sounds that were filling the kitchen just driving me on further.

"Trevor," she groaned louder, trembling under me. "Oh my god. It's too much…" she broke off, my hand flexing around her throat.

"You can take it." I panted against her ear. "It's not too much. It's not ever going to be enough, Monica. Fuck, baby." I released her hand and wrapped it around the front of her, to the apex of her thighs. My fingers found her clit circling it gently with steady pressure.

Her thighs were shaking as her pussy clenched around me, tightening, as she took sobbing breaths under me.

"You going to cum for me?" I asked, pressing firmer against her clit.

"Yes, please, Trev." she was crying out now, both hands trying to find purchase on the counter, I gripped her hips, releasing her neck, angling her to fuck into her harder and deeper.

"Cum on my cock, Monica." I growled as she screamed under me, her pussy gripping me tight as her orgasm took over her body.

I kept thrusting, feeling my own body tense, emptying into her, curving over her again, kissing over her upper back and shoulders as we both panted.

Gently, I stepped back, pulling myself out of her, looking down to see us mixed together. Reaching up I collected some of my cum sliding out of her, and pushed it back into her, pressing my finger deep inside.

She moaned softly, whispering my name, her forehead pressed against the counter and everything was perfect.

CHAPTER EIGHTEEN

MONICA

Everything was perfect. Or it should be. I rolled my heated forehead against the cool kitchen counter. I was still trembling and my legs were unsteady. I felt Trevor's hands soothing my back, his callouses rasping against the skin.

Being with Trevor again had been amazing. Perfect. I'd seen stars. So why did I feel like I was going to burst into tears? Why was Paul's face the one I was seeing behind my closed eyes? I felt like I had just cheated on my husband, even though I knew that wasn't the case.

My breathing was starting to hitch as I straightened my body, my skin meeting Trevor's hard chest behind me, as his arms came around me holding me gently.

"You okay?" He asked against my ear, sounding concerned.

"Yep." My voice sounded off, even to myself. I needed to get to the bathroom and pull myself together. Trevor didn't need this and I felt ready to shatter apart.

"I gotta run to the restroom, just give me a second." I said, voice thin with false bravado. I avoided his eyes as I turned, scooping my clothes up, and rushing over to the bathroom. My breath was starting to come in bursts and I felt like my chest was caving in.

I'd never had a panic attack but this is what I imagined one felt like. Closing and locking the door behind me, I thrust my hand into the shower, turning the water on to create noise right before I hit my knees outside of the bathtub. The clothes I'd scooped up fell to the floor and I started wheezing.

I hadn't cheated on Paul. It had been a year and a half since he'd passed. Why was my mind reacting this way? I'd been in the moment with Trevor. I'd had one of the best orgasms of my life. Then the come down had hit me. Everything had hit me again.

I heard myself start sobbing just as the first tears hit my hands.

Pull it together. God, please.

Everything felt like it was tunneling out and I laid on my side, curled into a ball. The cool tiles of the bathroom floor jarred against the steam enveloping the bathroom from the water running.

I was going to break.

Distantly, I heard knocking on the door and Trevor's voice, but I was so panicked I couldn't register what he was saying. I had never been this delicate flower. I felt guilty about Paul and guilty I had run right after Trevor and I had sex.

There was pounding now and near panicked shouting. He had to hear me sobbing but I couldn't breathe. The bathroom door banged open, slamming against the wall, cool air rushing in to cover my body that was draped in steamy condensation from the heated shower.

"Fuck, Mon."

I felt Trevor step over me, crouching, then sliding behind me to sit on the floor. Then he was pulling me up as I was trying to pull away, pull myself together for him. So he didn't think it was because of him. But he fought me.

My back came against his bare chest as he held each of my wrists, crossing mine and his arms over my chest and holding me tight against him.

"Breathe." His voice was rough. "Feel my chest moving against you and match my breaths." He ordered, holding me even tighter. He hadn't even turned the water off. Just focusing on getting to me, holding himself against me, and providing a port in this storm.

"I'm sorry," I started, my voice shaky, thin and breathless.

"Shut the fuck up and breathe, Monica," he demanded. "You have nothing to be sorry for. Absolutely nothing. I can't imagine what you're feeling after your first…after having sex for the first time…" even he kept breaking off.

He seemed unsure of what to say, what to bring up, that wouldn't cause me to spiral further into the panic, instead of settling into the calm he was trying to provide.

"I'm here for it all. You can't keep running from me. I thought I'd hurt you or something." He was speaking softly now, as my breaths stopped racing and I gradually relaxed against him. He moved a hand up, releasing one of my wrists, and soothed it against my hair.

"I'd be shocked if you hadn't had some kind of emotions after this." He continued, "Fuck. I'm having emotions. He was my friend too, Monica. He was like a brother. He helped save me…", his voice broke.

I turned to face him and wrapped my arms around him, drawing him closer to me.

"Just don't keep running from me. Let me help, baby. Let me walk through this with you. When you can't walk anymore, let me carry you. Let me fight the pain with you."

I pressed my face against his neck, he was still naked. There was something very primal about this kind of grief. Both of us without clothes, wrapped around each other, healing.

"I don't know what happened," I tried to explain, my voice trembling. "It wasn't you or what we did. It was amazing. It just hit me…" I continued.

His hands moved up, pulling me back and cradling my face gently, green eyes scorching into mine. He looked fierce.

"And when that happens you don't shove me out. My love for you isn't fragile, Monica. I know you loved Paul. I know this was a huge step. I'd have held you on the kitchen floor, the middle of the street, a crowded restaurant. Fuck, baby. Whenever you need me and wherever it hits you. I'm there. I'd walk through fire to get to you if you were hurting and needed me."

I hiccuped a soft sob, more tears escaping my eyes, as he brought his forehead against mine and we breathed each other's oxygen.

"I know," I whispered, "I'm sorry."

"Stop fucking apologizing to me for things I'm supposed to help with." He growled, fingers tangling in my hair.

"I fucking love you, Monica. That will never change. That has never changed."

"I love you too," I spoke softly, bringing my hands to rest on his chest.

"Come here," he said, standing and bringing me up with him, holding me steady. Stepping into the shower, he pulled me in gently behind him.

"Let me take care of you," he continued, guiding me under the water and running his fingers through my hair. "Let yourself be taken care of. You don't have to be so strong all the goddamn time."

So I let him. I willed my body to relax and let him gently wash my hair. Shampooing and rinsing it with more care than I did myself every day. He worked conditioner through the strands with gentleness instead of the harsh tugs I gave myself in the mornings.

As his hands roamed over my body with soap I felt myself coming down from the emotions of everything.

The nerves of coming here tonight.

Having sex with someone new for the first time in fourteen years.

The panic attack.

As he rinsed me off and held me, I laid my head against his chest, weary and drained. I felt like a vase that could be tipped over and broken at any moment. Bare and exposed. Groggy.

He turned the water off and stepped out, guiding me again. He wrapped a towel that smelled like him around me and used another to dry my hair gently before combing it. It was like he could sense I needed his presence but no words.

His eyes kept meeting mine in the bathroom mirror and all I could see there was love and concern. I felt safer and more taken care of than I had in a long time. He'd grown into an amazing man.

He took my hand and gently pulled me through the apartment to his bedroom. The king-size bed took up the majority of the room, and pulled the covers back.

He took the wet towels off of me and guided me to lay down and crawled in behind me. Covering us both he pulled me back, so that I was tight against him, wrapping me in his arms.

"Rest, Mon," he soothed, kissing the back of my head, "I've got you."

CHAPTER NINETEEN
RICHARD

I was glaring at my son, standing in front of me, wringing his hands like some sort of fucking pansy.

"Jackson. This isn't rocket science. All I need is information. Bait. What the fuck is your problem?" I growled.

"I just don't think it's right. They're good people."

My fist clenched around the lighter in my hand.

"Fine." I said, my voice darkening.

"Fine?" He asked, disbelieving.

"You had your chance to do it your way. Now I'm going to do it myself."

My response seemed to alarm him. Go figure. Bleeding hearts and all that bullshit.

"You can't hurt Lacey, Dad."

I smirked, leaning forward on our sagging couch in the trailer.

"I won't hurt her, son. Intentionally. But no one can say what may result in collateral damage."

"Wait—"

"Shut the fuck up and get out of my house, Jackson. You had your chance. Unless you're willing to start hitting the streets for me, leave. And you can forget the fucking college payments."

I scowled at his back as he slammed the door behind him.

At least I was rid of that pussy finally. No son of mine anymore.

I kicked the folding table in front of me sending drugs and paraphernalia flying.

Picking up my cell phone I dialed the number I needed.

"Mike? Mhmm. On to Plan B."

CHAPTER TWENTY
TREVOR

Monica had scared the shit out of me last night. I was laying in my bed, holding her, the sun barely rising outside the window.

I stared at the pink and purplish light of dawn playing through her dark brunette strands. Maybe I should've held back. Neither of us were the same people we'd been when we were young. She'd been with another man for a long time.

Maybe she thought I expected her to just bounce back to how we'd always connected. I should've taken her to bed and done things properly. I was seriously despising myself in the light of day.

"Trevor. I can feel you thinking." Monica's voice, raspy with sleep, startled me. She turned, wiggling around until her brown eyes met mine sleepily.

"You can't keep things from me either, you know. This is a two way street."

Touching her cheek softly, I began, "I'm just sorry about last night. I wanted you so badly that I wasn't thinking. I should've taken my time, brought you to bed—"

"Shut up." She said, covering my mouth. "I was literally begging you for it. It was amazing. It wasn't you, Trev. It was the emotions of the situation as a whole."

"Are you sure? I thought I'd hurt you, Mon. Even if it was just emotionally—"

"I said shut up. I already ruined the experience with my meltdown last night." She sighed.

"You shut up. You didn't ruin anything." I leaned forward kissing her softly. "I love you. I'm here no matter what you're feeling. You're perfect." I spoke close to her mouth, letting my lips brush hers as I did so.

Her hand wrapped around my shoulder and pulled me closer, pressing her lips harder against mine. She slid her tongue along the seam of my lips until I parted mine. I stroked against her gently sucking, before pulling away.

"Better watch it, woman. You're gonna start something." I smirked.

"That was the plan, smart ass." She sassed back at me.

"Oh ya?" I raised up on my elbow, pushing her onto her back, pulling the blankets off of us. Her body came into view. Soft and inviting. And she let me look, less shy than the night before. She teasingly stretched her arms over her head, arching her back, and pushing her breasts out, nipples hardening.

"I want you, Trev. That was never our problem."

I placed my large hand on her chest, between her breasts. Her breathing picked up, just at the simplest touch. It almost took my breath away that she was in front of me again like this.

Mine.

I moved my hand down her chest to her stomach. Watching my tanned skin against her paler softness. My tattoos were startling against her. My own breathing picked up as she whimpered softly.

"Spread your legs, baby" I ordered, voice gravelly.

She wiggled impatiently and parted them, raising and bending her knees to let them fall open wide. Baring herself to me. I raised up onto my knees, moving between her legs, and growled at the sight before me.

"Fuck. Are you always this wet for me?" I rasped, pushing her knees apart wider with my hands.

"Always," she whispered, breathless.

I trailed the pointer finger of my right hand down the seam of her pussy as she moaned again.

"Trevor," she pleaded.

"What do you want, Monica?" I asked, pushing my finger inside her to the knuckle and twisting my hand. She arched under me, gasping.

"More…You…Everything." She pleaded, her eyes falling shut.

"Open those eyes. Put them on me and keep them there, or I stop."

Her eyes flew open meeting mine as I pulled my finger out and brought it up to my lips, sucking her off of me, moaning.

"You taste amazing."

Her hands gripped the sheets on either side of her.

"Trevor. Fuck."

"I love when you're frustrated and desperate for me." I smirked at her, "remember to keep those eyes on me."

I brought myself down to my stomach between her splayed legs, and covered her with my mouth. Sucking the wetness off of her, lapping at her with my tongue.

She cried out, as I looked up into her eyes, she was struggling to keep them open and on mine.

"Having trouble keeping those pretty browns on me, beautiful?" I asked before I drove my tongue as far inside of her as I could fucking get with it.

"Ass." She muttered, gasping.

I slowly moved my lips up, sealing them around her clit, sucking hard, maintaining eye contact.

I watched her eyes roll back in her head as her legs wrapped around my head. I was in heaven. I could die happy right here between this woman's thighs. I slid two fingers inside her, curling them against her front wall, finding her g-spot, rubbing it firmly.

I relished in the fact that she started shaking, gripping me tighter, as she yelled my name, staring into my eyes desperately. She was already close, and I knew it.

I loved it.

I loved that I could control her body like this.

I sucked harder pressing my face tighter against her, as her hips started bucking against my mouth, as she whimpered and cried out.

"Fuck. Fuck. Fuck. Trevor! I'm going to—"

I growled against her clit, pressing my fingers into her inner wall harder against that spot, and she shattered around me.

She looked fucking gorgeous, and I kept lapping at her eagerly, rocking my hand with my fingers inside her as she came apart, while her hips writhed and she rode her orgasm to the end. She was taking sobbing breaths as her body slowly stilled, legs falling from where they were wrapped around my neck.

"Oh my, God," she gasped, as I moved up her body and over her, kissing her lips and stealing the breath she was trying to catch. I reached down gripping the base of my shaft, and slid inside her halfway, pulling back, and smirking down at her.

"You're trying to kill me," she groaned as I drove the rest of the way inside her, our pelvises meeting and grinding my hips in a circle.

"Oh my God, that piercing," she moaned, arching up into me.

"Nice addition, huh?" I asked, bracing my hands on either side of her head and drawing back to plunge in again all the way.

"Trevor!" She cried out, wrapping her legs around me along with her arms.

"That's it, baby," I rasped, "Hold on, tight."

CHAPTER TWENTY ONE
MONICA

Trevor was going to fuck me to death. As he drove back inside of me my entire body shook against him. I found myself uncontrollably raking my nails down his back as he growled approvingly. He looked like a predator, braced over me, staring at my face intently.

He owned me entirely in this moment and I was relishing it. I wanted him to take me. I moved my hips against his, meeting him thrust for thrust, feeling his piercing grazing against my walls deep inside.

It sent electricity through my body and I couldn't control the sounds coming out of my mouth. I was being loud and it was early in the morning in an apartment building but fuck if I cared.

"That's it, baby. Take every inch of this cock inside that pussy and own it. Scream my name so my neighbors know who's fucking you and making you feel this good." He panted against my mouth before taking my lips in a searing kiss.

The mouth on this man.

I broke the kiss, practically screaming his name, my entire body trembling and shaking.

"Trevor, I'm going to come again," I gasped as he drove into me harder, a drop of sweat falling off of his forehead onto my mouth.

I licked my lips, tasting the saltiness and he growled watching me. His hand found my throat and squeezed right.

"That's fucking right you are." He groaned, "Come all over your cock, Monica. This is your cock. Be a good girl and come for me."

And I shattered again. Everything went white in my vision as my body convulsed, wrapping around him tight to hold onto something.

I felt him thrusting and tightening above me until he erupted inside of me deep, pulsing rhythmically, still gripping my neck.

"Fuck, Monica. Fuck." He stared down at me when I blinked my eyes open. His blonde hair was in his eyes and he looked glorious and completely taken apart over me.

"Well," I said, clearing my throat. "We still have really hot sex." I reached up, running my fingers through his hair. "And you have an absolutely filthy mouth."

He barked a laugh, gripping my wrist and turning my hand to kiss my palm.

"Fuck. I love you." He said, laughing.

"I love you too, Trevor." I smiled.

. . . .

A few hours later, after I'd showered and left Trevor's apartment, I was knocking on Becks' door when she answered.

"You don't look too good." I stated, concerned. She was still in her pajamas and looked like she'd barely slept. I handed her the to-go cup of hot tea I'd picked up on the way.

"Come in." She stated, avoiding eye contact. I watched as she took the cup, her hand trembling, and led the way into the house. She was making my concern grow by the minute.

"Becks? What the hell is the matter?" I asked, reaching out to grab my friend's arm and stop her.

"Nothings really wrong, Mon. We just had an issue with Lacey—"

"Oh, for the love of God." I put my iced coffee down on the wooden table in the middle of the living room, exasperated.

"What did she do now?" I asked, feeling my blood pressure rise.

"Lucas was coming downstairs to get me a glass of water in the kitchen around three this morning, and caught her letting Jackson in the back door."

I stared at Becks completely stunned.

"What?!" I exclaimed.

"It's not as bad as you think. Just let me get Lucas to help. We didn't want to call you all in the middle of the night. He heard Jackson out and got onto them both pretty hard. Especially the fact that Jackson is nineteen and Lacey just turned seventeen. LUCAS!" she yelled towards the back of the house where their bedroom was. She still wouldn't make eye contact and my stomach was clenching with trepidation.

I dropped to the couch, stunned, my hand meeting my forehead. I checked my phone. Nine a.m.

"You could've called sooner—"

"Mon." Becks cut me off as Lucas walked into the room behind her seat. "It was the middle of the night and other than her trying to let him in to talk nothing horrific happened."

I just stared at them both, still trying to come to terms with my oldest daughter's behavior.

Lucas placed his tattooed arm along the back of the couch behind his wife and smiled reassuringly at me.

"Really, Monica. Just hear me out first." His familiar voice was deep and comforting.

"Okay," I said, "Hit me."

"The kids told me they were just meeting to talk. And, Mon, I gotta tell you I believe them. Jackson always seemed to have his shit together. He was heavily involved in sports and got good grades in high school. He has even been trying to go to college. He said his father has been blackmailing him for information on Trevor. Trying to get him to use Lacey. He was coming to tell her that he kept refusing. His dad cut him loose last night. Disowned him for refusing to help or sell drugs for him."

"That is disgusting!" I exclaimed, immediately furious with the man for treating his child like that.

First, he'd taken my first husband and Lacey's dad from me, stealing precious years, now he was using my daughter and his son?

Lucas leaned in to speak softer.

"I'm gonna need you to stay calm. But he also said his father had some rather unflattering things to say about myself, Becks, and even Paul. Apparently he knew and was a big fan of fucking Larry."

My entire body tensed at the name as I watched my best friend's face pale. She turned as white as a sheet and wrapped her arms around herself. Suddenly, her actions when I'd gotten here made sense.

"I'm so sorry, Monica. I brought all this onto you guys and everything's happened because of me—"

I waved my hand, cutting her off as Lucas tried to rub her back reassuringly.

"Becks. None of this is your fault. I told you that over a year ago and I'm telling you that now." I met her eyes intently, willing her to believe me.

"I love you. You're like the sister I never had. I would never blame you for this."

"See, babe? That's exactly what I told you she'd say." Said the man beside her, gentler than I'd ever seen him. You could see the concern written all over his face as his eyes scanned his wife's drawn and pale face.

"She didn't sleep at all after all that and has been incredibly stressed. She made herself sick twice."

"Becks!" I exclaimed, worriedly. I rose and came around to her other side, gripping her hand tightly.

"This isn't your fault." I repeated.

"I know. I'm just emotional and anxious and the pregnancy hormones—" her voice broke off tearfully.

I pulled her into a hug, worriedly meeting Lucas' gaze. This kind of stress couldn't be good for her or the baby when she already has anxiety and PTSD.

Lucas picked up the hot tea, holding it carefully in his large tattooed hand, and pressed it into her, urging her to take small sips.

"It's decaf and sweet. Just the way you've been liking it." I said, watching her. "You need to relax."

I looked back at Lucas.

"So…what do we do now?" I asked.

"Well. It's all heresy and he's been flying under the radar since his last run in with us. Richard is tough. We can never pin anything on him. All we can really do is monitor him and his accomplices. I've set Jackson up somewhere safe for now. He's gonna stay with Nick. Find a job. Try to get back into school and even the dorms with some financial aid since his dad is a dick. But I really think this is what's been up with Lacey's attitude. She's been worried about Jackson, she lost Paul, she's going into her senior year—"

"It makes sense. That's a lot for anyone, let alone a seventeen-year-old. I just wish she'd come to me. She always talked to Paul when she was stressed though." I said, nodding. "Jesus. It's always something anymore." I scrubbed my hands over my face. "I need to tell Trevor." I whispered.

"I texted him. I was thinking about grilling tonight. Having all of you over anyway. We can all talk then. Have the kids entertain each other. He said it was good with him if it was okay with you." Lucas suggested.

"I was gonna get Becks some breakfast and make her lay down and sleep a while. Take Nat to do something. Give her time to calm down and breathe."

He still only had eyes for his wife, the concern palpable and radiating off of him. Becks still struggled to lean on anyone else for help when she felt like this.

Becks rolled her dark eyes at him as he narrowed his gray ones at her.

I smirked, "That all sounds perfect. Including getting this pregnant mama some sleep and food." I stressed, glaring at my best friend.

"But I think you should stay with her and I should take Nat

with the girls to the pool for the afternoon." I added.

Lucas looked at me gratefully even as Becks started to argue.

"Shut up," her husband and I both said together, cutting her off before she could fight us.

It was going to be a good day after all. I was determined.

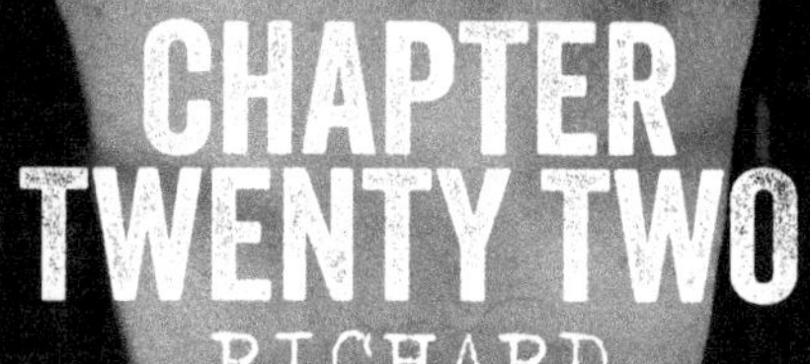

CHAPTER TWENTY TWO
RICHARD

"We play the long game." I spoke softly, staring across the booth in the seedy bar we frequented. Mike and Chuck stared back at me with bloodshot eyes. No one really kept too close of tabs on them. Nondescript and oily. The better people of this town liked to pretend we didn't exist.

I raised a finger to the waitress passing to signal another round. The owner typically let us drink on the house, we provided him the poison of his choice frequently.

Tina, or whatever-the-fuck-her-name was, nodded at me and winked. The neon lights advertising different alcohol selections not providing a kind light on her features. She was past her prime and used up. She'd probably been pretty once. Not any more. Whatever. One of us would be able to get our dick wet with her tonight. Or maybe we'd share her.

"What if your boy is with them?" Chuck asked quietly, his eyes on the point of his pocket knife digging into our usual table.

He was leaving quite a mark after all these years. No one had the balls to say anything though.

"I don't have a boy any more." I growled.

Mike laughed while Chuck's eyes gleamed in understanding.

"I don't give a fuck who gets caught in the crossfire." I slapped the waitress's ass as she set our drinks down and walked away.

"I just want Trevor Connor to pay."

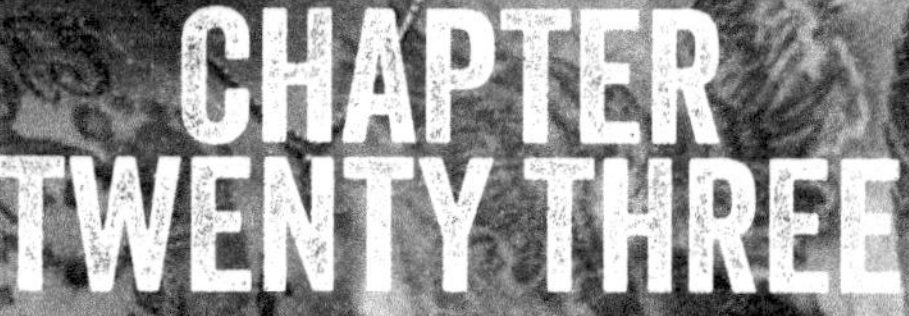

CHAPTER TWENTY THREE
TREVOR

I stared at Lucas across the kitchen of his house. He'd just finished filling me in on everything that had happened with Lacey and Jackson the night before.

Monica and Becks were sitting on the back patio visiting. Mon was trying to keep Becks calm, still worried about how stressed and nervous she'd been earlier.

I heard the girls playing music loudly upstairs as my friend took a bottle of beer and a bottle of water out of the fridge and passed me the latter.

"And you all can't fucking do anything?" I asked, screwing the lid off angrily and tossing it on the counter.

"We literally only have Jackson's words against his father's, Trevor," came Lucas' low voice.

I took a drink and set it on the counter, hands flat on either side, staring at the clear water inside of the bottle.

"Do I need to do something?" I asked, my voice sounding

brittle, even to my own ears.

"Like what, Trev? Get yourself killed or in trouble again? You think Monica or those girls need that? Man, I know what it's like holding yourself back. I put up a helluva fight when it involved Becks and Nat. Ask Nick. He's the one I threw up against a wall. But, they've been through a lot of shit. They don't need to lose you too."

I glared over at him, green eyes meeting brown.

"I know these men, Lucas."

"I know you do. These women are stronger than we think. They have us. Fuck. Becks handled her own shit with Clark and Larry. I barely got to lay hands on them. It's not going to come to that. I need you to hold your shit together for me. Let us handle this. Keep your nose clean. We don't need you dead or locked up, dumbass." he called me the name jokingly, but the seriousness of his tone was far from a joke.

I looked at the back of Monica's head outside sitting by Becks. Both of them had their hair up in those damn buns women were wearing, laughing at each other. I couldn't lose this woman again. I wouldn't lose this woman again.

"Fine." I answered, voice clipped. "But if it comes to me when I'm with them, they're mine."

"Understood." He tapped his bottle against mine and we both drank. Some primal understanding that we would protect what was ours to protect, no fucks given on the consequences.

"So, Jackson is staying with Nick?" I asked changing the subject, leading Lucas back outside.

"Yep. Agreed without complaint. He's in that old house all by himself. One nineteen-year-old kid, who's just using it as somewhere to sleep and study, isn't gonna bother him."

"I think it'll be good for him," came Becks' soft voice. She leaned over automatically, into Lucas as he put an arm around her. "He seems so lonely."

I barked out a laugh.

"Nick likes being alone." I replied.

"No. I know what she means. Nick may talk a big game, but he seems sad." said Monica beside me.

"Oh, God. The women have found their next project." Lucas groaned as Becks swatted him. "Should we warn him?"

"Nah, let him figure out he's fucked on his own, man." I replied, laughing and drawing Monica close to me as night settled in.

"Promise me you'll call if you need anything at all?" I looked over at Monica. Lacey and Lexi had said goodnight and ran into the house. I was headed back to my place.

"I don't think the girls would mind if I started staying here." I added, worriedly.

Mon grinned at me and shook her head.

"Trevor. We will be fine. If anything happens I will call you. I was a cop's wife forever. I do know a little self-defense anyway."

I chilled, thinking of her alone and having to defend herself and those girls.

"Trev, stop." her palm met my cheek, gently. "Nothing is going to happen, hon."

I tried to smile and failed. I knew it didn't reach my eyes. Nodding, I leaned over and kissed her.

"Text me when you get home. I love you." she said, kissing

me back, before climbing out. I watched her round the front of my truck, waving at me in the glare of the headlights. I had half a mind to sleep in my truck out here tonight. Fuck what anyone thought. But Monica would have my ass if I did that.

I waved back, watching until she shut the door behind her and flicked the lights, letting me know it was locked. Reversing, I pulled out onto the street and headed to my lonely apartment by myself. I knew I'd be lying awake all night worrying about my girls. Lucas could run his mouth about understanding all he wanted.

I knew he was a cop and as such had seen some of the worst humanity had to offer. But I'd lived it for my entire life. I didn't want it touching Monica, Lacey, or Lexi any more than it already had. They didn't deserve it. I'd brought enough into their lives back when I'd chosen to walk out that door.

Driving across town the angry rock music I was known for wasn't doing anything for my mood. When I reached the parking lot, I turned the truck off and sat in the silence, pondering.

Monica could fight it all she wanted right now. But tomorrow I was going to start hounding her to let me move in. Those three girls didn't need to be alone in a big house with this kind of threat going around. I felt bad for Jackson. Apparently he was more like me than I'd realized. Being raised by drug-addled parents. Trying to rise above and do better than that. Fuck. I needed to talk to the kid myself. I hadn't left a very good impression when I'd stood glaring at him in the hospital after the wreck.

Sighing, I got out and locked my truck before I heard a voice speak.

"Beautiful night out, isn't it, Trevor?"

I pocketed my keys calmly and turned, meeting Mike's in the

glow of the parking lot's lights.

"It was." I answered, voice clipped, short.

"You live in this building?" he asked, trying to play off the conversation like we were old friends and I knew he wasn't scouting for information.

"I think you already know the answer to that question. Let's not play dumb." I took several long strides to stand toe to toe with him. "What can I help you with?"

"Just saw an old friend. Wanted to visit."

"Bull shit."

"Watch yourself, Trevor. When Richard isn't happy…well we all know what happens when Richard isn't happy." he smirked, turning and walking away into the darkness.

My blood was pumping, nerves shot. I was barely restraining myself from going after him and pummeling his sorry ass. Threat received. I heard them loud and clear. Monica didn't have a choice at this point. Either I moved in with her tomorrow, or they all crammed into my two bedroom apartment. I didn't give a fuck.

I took my phone out of my pocket and called her.

"Trevor, you literally just left here. Stop." she said, her voice coming across the line teasingly.

"I just had a visitor." I stated abruptly.

She stopped laughing.

"Who? Richard?" she asked, concern dripping from her voice. "Trevor, are you okay?"

"I'm fine. But this situation isn't anymore, Monica. It wasn't Richard. It was a friend of his. I'm moving in there or you're moving in here tomorrow. I'll sleep on the couch. I don't give a fuck what it takes. You're not staying alone with all this shit going on and those two girls—"

"Okay."

Her voice stopped me.

"Okay?" I asked, somewhat disbelievingly. I thought she'd stomp her foot and throat a fit.

"Yes. Trevor, move in here tomorrow." she spoke, soft. "The girls know we're together and knew it was coming. This is scary. They've already been through too much. There's strength in numbers, right?"

"Right. I'll pack a bag and be back over in a few minutes. We'll come get the rest of my shit later tomorrow."

She sighed. I could almost envision her rolling her eyes on the other end of the line.

"Fine." she whispered. "I'll go tell the girls. But, no details. Lexi doesn't need to be terrified and Lacey is already stressed, we all know."

"Deal. I love you, see you in a few."

"Love you."

CHAPTER TWENTY FOUR
MONICA

Three Months Later

"LACEY! YOU SAID I COULD BORROW IT!"

My eyes met Trevor's across the kitchen table.

"Bet you didn't sign up for this when you demanded to move in three months ago." I chuckled at him.

He raised his eyebrow, shaking his hair out of his eyes.

"You don't like all the orgasms I've been giving you every night?" he asked, voice low.

I felt my cheeks heat. *This man.*

"Girls!" I yelled to deflect as Trevor smirked knowingly at me. "We don't need this argument every morning this school year!" I shook my head.

One month into the new school year and they were having the same fight every day.

In a lapse of her better judgment, Lacey had told Lexi she could borrow some tops occasionally. Lexi in excitement had attempted to do this daily, without checking what her older sister wanted to wear. Lacey had been acting so much better since we'd found out everything she was dealing with on her own. She'd resorted back to the more typical teenage angst you could expect out of someone her age. She was still nervous about her senior year. But I felt like she was going to be able to enjoy it more.

Jackson had settled into Nick's house and started the new semester at the local college. His financial aid came through for classes but not housing, so Nick had just decided to let him stay. He brushed it off as nothing but I knew it meant the world to Jackson. He'd needed a stable male figure in his life. Lucas, Trevor, and Nick were providing something like that for him for the first time in his life.

We hadn't heard anything else out of Mike, Chuck, or Richard since the threat in Trevor's old apartment's parking lot. It was eerie. We all chalked it up to them talking shit and not having the balls to follow through. Trevor said it was probably because they spent too much of their time high and selling drugs to plan anything.

We'd settled into a peaceful routine. I was secretly grateful for the shove it gave us with Trevor moving in. I felt like it was meant to be. He had started out on the couch, trying to keep up pretenses for the girls. Until Lacey had smarted off one morning after two weeks of him doing this that she and Lexi both knew he was sneaking into my room at night.

I'd been horrified, Trevor had blushed like he used to in high school. Lacey and Lexi had been hysterical. It was wonderful to watch them with him. They'd missed Paul and his antics so much, having a man around was healing for them. It was healing for me.

I felt like all of our grief came in waves still, but it was together. We all had our bad days, missing our father, husband, and friend, but we were all there for each other too.

Footsteps thundered down behind us as Lacey swung around into the kitchen from the stairs.

"Little sisters are annoying." She growled, heading straight for the coffee machine.

Trevor snorted quietly, and looked up from his cereal.

"She's all you in the morning, babe." he laughed.

"Shut up," I sassed, still cranky myself. I'd only had one cup of coffee. Lacey had obviously inherited her need for caffeine before dealing with people from me.

Trevor's eyes heated as he looked at me.

"What did I tell you last night?" he asked softly.

I blushed, staring behind me to make sure Lacey was preparing her travel mug of coffee for school. Trevor had informed me that the next time I told him to shut up he'd shut my mouth up with something of his last night. I stared at him pointedly as he raised his eyebrows, uncaring that our daughter was in the room.

"That's what I thought." he said as I kicked him under the table. "You'll pay for that tonight," he promised.

"UNCLE LUCAS AND AUNT BECKS ARE HERE!" screamed Lexi as she tore down the stairs and headed to the front door. Lucas had promised to drive Lacey to her school today while Becks and I drove where I worked and Nat and Lexi attended.

The school had hired Becks to organize the front office this fall and create a more accurate filing system. She was geeked out over it. I loved getting to work with her every day while the project was ongoing. I smiled as my best friend walked into the room with her burly husband following her.

Becks' hand rested on her stomach. She was showing now at seven months along. They'd had a gender reveal the previous month and we'd all found out it was a boy. They refused to share a name with us though.

"How are you doing, mama?" I asked, standing and moving to hug her.

"Tired." she groaned. "Why is growing a tiny human so exhausting?"

Lucas was watching her carefully again and I raised an eyebrow at him over her shoulder, questioningly.

He shook his head.

I'd make him tell me later.

"The miracle of life is amazing. You're amazing, Becks." said Trevor.

"Amazing my ass. I feel like a cow." said Becks, sitting in a kitchen chair and pouting. "I want coffee."

Lucas rolled his eyes, "I told you the doctor said you could have a little. It's not going to hurt him. You chose to cut out caffeine."

"Shut up and stop reminding me of that." Becks scowled at him.

"Bad move, Lucas," I said, moving over to get my friend a mug for her favorite tea I kept stocked. "Do not anger it."

"It?" snarked Becks. "Should I be offended?" She directed the question to Trevor. "My best friend and husband are picking on me."

"I'll always be on your side, Becks." Trevor promised, as she nodded appreciatively. "It's safer from the hormones that way." he added as Becks threw a magazine from the table at him.

"Jerks." she muttered.

"So, how did yesterday's appointment go?" I asked, setting the mug in front of my friend.

"Good," said Becks.

"Becks." growled Lucas. She sighed, glaring, when I looked over at him. "The doctor is worried about her blood pressure. Becks has been told to keep calm and take it easy so she doesn't end up delivering the little man before he's done baking."

"Becks!" I said, "That's something you should probably tell us." I scolded.

"I don't want to be babied." she whined. "I took care of myself fine with Nat."

"Did you have high blood pressure with Nat? Did you have me when you were pregnant with Nat? Did you have friends when you were pregnant with Nat?" Lucas ranted, hands on his uniformed hips, eyes on his wife.

I watched my friend tear up. I understood it was still hard for her to concede and accept help and peoples' presence in her life.

"Okay." I said. "Lucas, you need to get Lacey to school. I know what's going on and I am working with Becks now. I got her, big guy."

He sighed, and looked at me gratefully. Striding over he ducked close to Becks' ear and whispered something I couldn't hear. I watched her sniffle and nod.

"I know, I love you too." she whispered. Lucas kissed her head before standing and nodding at me.

"Need a ride to the station?" he asked Trevor.

"If Mon can pick me up after work, sure."

"Oh great. The cop and the fireman are taking me to school." groaned my oldest behind me as Nat and Lexi came bounding down the stairs.

I snorted, hugging Lacey tight.

"Enjoy it. I love you. Have a good day."

"Love you too, Mom." I watched her, Lucas, and Trevor walk out the door after Trevor kissed me goodbye.

"Girls, in the car!" I ordered the younger ones as they ran through the kitchen with their backpacks. I stood staring at my best friend as she looked back at me.

"Ready to kick this day's ass?" I asked, helping her to her feet.

CHAPTER TWENTY FIVE

TREVOR

"So, things are still going well over on your end with Mon?" Lucas looked over at me, briefly glancing before returning his eyes to the road. We'd just dropped Lacey off at school and had each barely gotten a wave out of her. Lucas had made sure to blow a kiss at her and yell her name to thoroughly antagonize her. I'd be amused if I'd known I wasn't going to be the one going home to the repercussions later.

"Everything is good on our end. We still haven't seen or heard anything from Richard and company. Anything on y'all's? Surely they've gotten citations for something. They've never gone this long without one of them serving some kind of time."

"There hasn't been anything. It's creepy as hell because you're right. We're usually bringing one of the jackasses in on some kind of charge. Or we get a complaint about something they've done."

"Nick is still doing well with Jackson living with him?" I asked. I'd spoken to Jackson and gotten a feel for the kid. He really reminded me of myself. Part of me was terrified because I'd been like a magnet to Monica at that age. Lacey didn't really seem interested as more than a friend though, and neither did he. He came over for the occasional barbeque at one of our houses but most of the time kept busy with studies and his part time job he'd found.

"They're doing great. If it makes sense, it's like Nick has some sort of purpose now. He doesn't seem so gloomy." laughed Lucas, pulling into the fire station to drop me off.

"That's good though. We can't tell Monica and Becks. They'll never let us hear the end of it. Them being right and all that."

"No shit." smirked Lucas, throwing his truck into park. "We'll see you all later tonight, right? For Nan's birthday?"

I nodded, grabbing my bag to jump out.

"Have a good day, sweetheart. I love you." he joked.

I punched his shoulder and climbed out of the truck shaking my head.

"You're such a jackass." I muttered, shutting the door. I hiked my duffle further up my shoulder as I heard Lucas pull away behind me. Looking up at the blue sky, I smiled. Things were going great, and this was going to be a wonderful day.

"Did you remember to grab the salad?"

"Mon, baby. I told you four times. It's in the backseat."

"Okay, okay. It's just, Lucas' Nan is intimidating. It's her birthday we're going to. They had me make the salad. Her favorite thing. This is nerve-wracking."

I started laughing as Monica fretted by my side and reached

over the console to lay one of my large hands on her thigh as I drove.

"Mon. That woman loves everyone. She wouldn't care if you forgot the salad. I promise she has the ingredients stocked in her kitchen at all times."

"Whatever." She laid her hand on top of mine and checked her phone.

"Becks wants to know our ETA." she continued.

"I'd say about ten minutes." I guessed, squeezing the inside of her leg as she slapped at me.

"Stop!" she exclaimed, dropping the phone into her bag. "Apparently Lucas got a call at the station and had to leave for a bit. We need to step on it. If that pregnant woman gets it in her head to climb on a stepstool Lucas is going to have all our asses."

I snorted and leaned forward to grab my phone as it rang.

"Damn. We're popular." I remarked.

"Hello?"

"Mr. Connor?"

"Jackson?" I listened to the kid clear his throat nervously. "What's up?"

"Well. I know it's stupid but I took the bus to the end of town and walked down to my dad's trailer. I was going to get something I forgot, but he showed up and won't let me leave. I was wondering if you knew where Nick was? He's not answering and I need a ride out of here."

I sighed, glancing over at Monica who was looking at me questioningly.

"Jackson." I mouthed quietly. I watched her eyebrows draw in, concerned.

"I think there's something going on down at the station,

Jackson. I can come get you."

"Oh. No, Trevor, that's okay. I'll try to walk."

"Jackson. It's not an issue. Just give me ten minutes." I could hear the fear and uncertainty in his voice and that was calling out to a younger version of myself. I hung up before he could fight me on the subject.

"What's going on?" asked Monica as I turned my truck onto a sidestreet to back up and return the way we came.

"He needs me to come get him. Apparently he remembered something he'd left behind and went to get it. His dad showed up and he needs a ride. Can't get a hold of Nick."

"Trevor. We should call Lucas."

"Mon. It's just Richard. For real. We'll pull up, let Jackson hop in, and take off. We're not going to start anything. Text Becks that it'll be a little longer."

Monica sighed and I had to admit a pit was settling in my stomach.

"Fine." she murmured.

I watched her out of the corner of my eye typing a text before she dropped her cell back into her bag.

"Is it all good?"

"She didn't answer. She probably set her phone down or Nat is on it or something. I sent the text though."

As I pulled down the gravel road leading back into the run-down lot that Richard had parked his trailer on, Monica spoke again, her voice shaky.

"Are you sure this is a good idea?"

"Mon. Nothing is going to happen. It's broad-fucking-day-light."

I watched the road ahead of us, as did Mon, suddenly seeing

smoke cresting the hill.

Drawing myself up to sit a little taller, we crested the top of the road leading down to where the trailer was.

Engulfed in flames, sitting in the middle of the field, against a bank of large overgrown trees and shrubs.

"Fuck. Call nine-one-one." I pressed my foot harder on the gas and gravel spun behind us as I took the road leading down to the trailer faster than was probably safe. Opening my door, I rolled to a stop, and glanced up to see Monica gaping at me.

"What the hell are you doing?" she asked. I saw her pulse pounding in her neck and her hands were shaking.

"Mon. I gotta make sure no ones actually in there. I'm a fire-fighter. Nothings going to happen. Tell the emergency operator the details."

I got further away from the truck hearing her speaking to someone on the phone. As I rounded the back, giving the trailer a wide berth with the intense heat coming off of it, I waved as the truck went out of my view the further I walked.

"Jackson!" I yelled.

This was a fucking inferno. If he and his father were inside, they weren't going to answer me. This didn't make any sense for the trailer to already be this engulfed in such a short amount of time. Things were not adding up. This fire had been set a while ago and left to burn.

I heard a noise behind me, but before I could spin to look, a sharp pain echoed through my skull, and all I saw was black.

Trevor had disappeared behind the burning trailer almost ten minutes ago. I thought he'd have circled it by now. The emergency personnel should be on their way, but I couldn't even hear sirens yet.

Climbing out of his huge truck, my stomach was churning and I felt like I was going to be sick. I could feel the heat from the flames from here. Maybe Trevor had been hurt?

"Mrs. Rodgers! RUN!" I heard someone yelling behind me, and I turned to meet Jackson's wide eyes as he tried to break free from the trees to the left that surrounded the back of the trailer. They'd be on fire soon themselves.

"Jackson?" I asked, panicked. I felt a motherly instinct to approach and protect, but a baser instinct to run and save myself. Trevor was back there somewhere though. I heard a bang and gasped, ducking and covering my head out of instinct.

Jackson's huge eyes stared at me one minute, then he was

facedown on the ground, the next. Some oily man standing behind him, that wasn't his father, came into view.

Terror flooded me and my entire body felt cold.

Run, Monica.

I could hear an inner voice screaming at me…Paul's voice screaming at me.

But, Trevor, where was Trevor?

I spun, sprinting towards the other side of the trailer, the way Trevor had gone, yelling for him as I redialed the emergency number on my cell.

"Someone's at the fire, they shot someone!" I gasped, as soon as I heard the voice on the phone. I wasn't even thinking straight or operating calmly. I was better than this. I had been a cop's wife for over a decade. I rounded the trailer, not seeing Trevor anywhere, a sob leaving my mouth as the woman tried to speak calmly to me.

Apparently, the woman had informed me they were patching me through to the police.

I heard Lucas Marshall's voice speak gruffly.

"What's the address of the emergency?"

"Lucas!?" I was screaming now, my adrenaline going crazy, spiking as I hit the treeline and kept running from the footsteps behind me.

"Monica? What the hell's going on?"

"They shot Jackson. They shot Jackson." I said, incapable of forming one coherent, complete thought.

"I don't know where Trevor went. We're on the Flinton prop-"

I smacked into a hard chest and fell backwards, landing on my back, the breath whooshing from my lungs.

"MONICA?!"

I could hear Lucas yelling from my cell phone and couldn't scramble fast enough to it. Someone placed a dark cloth over my face, a medicinal smell engulfed my senses, and everything went dark.

CHAPTER TWENTY SEVEN
TREVOR

My head was fucking killing me and I was infuriated. I'd returned to consciousness with my hands tied behind my back, and my legs tied to the legs of the chair I was in. I shook my hair out of my eyes and moved my wrists to try to loosen whatever was keeping them restrained. There was one lightbulb hanging from the ceiling and the air felt damp. I had to be in a basement somewhere. Obviously nowhere near the fire.

My heart was pounding wondering where I'd been taken, but panicking even more at the thought of Monica in that truck by herself. I'd essentially left her alone. I should've listened to her. I craned my neck trying to look behind me but everything was black. The lightbulb was barely hanging by its last threads and hardly illuminated the space around me. The only other light shone dimly through a small, dirty window across the room.

I grunted and kicked the bucket in front of me in frustration, and anger.

The noise echoed throughout the room and more light flooded in as a door opened at the top of, what I could now see were, the wooden stairs. A thumping echoed throughout the cellar-type area where I was. It was musty and cold. Two sets of feet were making their way down towards me, making noises as if they were struggling.

Rage built in me, simmering when I saw the source of their efforts.

Mike and Chuck were struggling their way down the rickety stairs. Chuck had Monica's arms caught under the shoulders while Mike gripped her knees, placing himself between her thighs and making his way backwards to the basement where I was. Just the image of her unconscious form and Mike's placement caused me to see red.

My wrists strained against the ropes tying them together, cursing

"Let her go right fucking now, assholes. Monica had nothing to do with this. I'll kill you both."

Chuck laughed at me as they both made it off the stairs. They let go, dropping Monica carelessly. I cringed watching her head bounce off the concrete floor. Grateful for the messy ponytail she'd thrown her brunette hair back in. Providing some cushion to the back of her head, she lay still, unmoving. I couldn't even tell if she was breathing because of the lighting and my heart rate picked up. My breaths were coming in rapid pants with my rising fury.

"Doesn't look like you're in a state to be killing anyone, Trevor." Mike said, turning and narrowing his dark eyes on my face.

"Looks like we can do whatever the fuck we want."

"What are y'all going to gain from this?" I asked, strategies switching. "All you've ever gone down for is theft and drug charges. You really wanna go down for kidnapping, arson, and causing harm? Murder? For what? Some small-town drug lord?"

"We got plans. Richard promised us. Something big's gonna—" Chuck started.

"Would you shut the fuck up, moron?" Mike warned through clenched teeth.

My eyes darted between them. Either Richard had fed his two minions a line of shit or something else was going down in Reading, Pennsylvania. I was just hoping Monica's call to nine-one-one had been enough to get someone out here immediately. Although, I wasn't sure where we even were anymore.

"Boss say what to do with the body?"

My muscles clenched, thinking they were talking about Monica.

"Just let me check her. Do whatever you want to me afterwards. Let me make sure she can't be helped." I begged, not too proud when it came to her life. I'd just gotten her back into mine and we hadn't had long enough.

Mike barked a rough laugh.

"Wrong body." he spoke coldly.

Brain racing, I just stared at them both. Wondering what other poor soul had been—

Jackson. Fuck.

"What the fuck did you two idiots do?" I yelled.

Chuck looked like he may say something, slight trepidation in his gaze as he took me in. Mike smacked him in the back of the head and pointed back up the stairs.

"We'll give you two some time alone." Grinned Mike, disappearing back up them behind his accomplice.

I heard the door shut with a slam, locks clicking into place.

Heavy footsteps echoed above me and my eyes trailed them on the ceiling, listening until another door opened and shut. Glancing around the basement again my stomach sank at what little there was to use around me.

My eyes shifted downward, taking in Monica's too still form.

"Monica," I urged. "Baby, please, wake up."

I heard a faint groan, sure I saw her shoulders raise and lower with a breath. Relief stole through me quickly as I took her in.

"Monica!" I hissed, louder. Terrified someone would hear me.

"Shut up." Monica groaned softly, hands coming up to her head. "I have a horrible headache, Trev. What—" her voice broke off and I knew she'd opened her eyes. Her brain coming back on board with the situation.

"Oh my God." she gasped, sitting up and swaying slightly.

"Are you okay?" I begged, my voice cracking.

Her panicked eyes met mine as she stood shakily.

"They didn't tie me up?" she questioned.

"Mon, baby, focus. Are you okay?"

"I think…" she was trembling all over. "They shot Jackson." her voice broke. "Right in front of me. I tried to run. They put some cloth over my face…I don't remember anything after that."

I clenched my teeth, my jaw groaning under the force.

I was going to kill anyone who'd had a hand in this.

"Listen. They probably didn't tie you up because they figure we can't get out of here. They locked the door when they went back upstairs. They don't want me loose because I'd fight them. But now that you're here they know I won't risk doing anything. You gotta untie me, Monica. I gotta get you out the window."

Her head jerked up, ponytail bouncing.

"*We* have to get out the window. *WE*, Trevor." she emphasized.

"Sure. We." I placated, knowing there was no way I was going to get out that tiny window with my frame. Monica may not even fit. Whatever I needed to tell her to get her out of here.

Monica hurried over, moving to my back, working at the knots they'd tied around my wrists. I felt them loosening and her fingers gently brushed over the places where I'd rubbed skin raw trying to get free.

I heard her sniffle as I bent untying my ankles so I could stand knowing she was close to breaking. I spared a minute, spinning to yank her into my arms, holding her tight, even for just a moment.

"It'll be okay. I'm going to get you out of this." I whispered. "I'm so sorry. I'm so sorry my choices brought this to your life."

Her hands worked between us, planting on my chest and shoving me backwards.

"Stop. You don't get to keep apologizing for other people's mistakes. You're getting out of here too." her eyes narrowed on my own. "I'm not leaving without you."

My fingers pinched her chin, tilting her head up.

"You're my priority. Getting you out and to your girls. *Our girls*. Is my priority. If you get out that window. You don't stop and you don't look around. You run. I'll work on getting to you. I made promises, Monica. I promised I'd keep you safe and keep those girls safe. You're my fucking priority. Don't argue with me about this."

Tears were trailing down her face, even as she shook her head. But I knew I'd won this battle. I knew she'd listen. Playing the highest card I had with a mother's children. She couldn't leave them orphans. They each couldn't lose two parents.

Turning, my eyes scanned the room, looking for anything useful. I saw the wall crumbling and walked over searching for a big enough piece of the cement they'd poured for walls.

"Stand back here." I ordered, walking over to the window. I peered up out of it, trying to gauge surroundings. Get a feel of where we were located. Drawing my arm back, I threw the cement through the window. As it shattered and glass flew my breath froze. Listening for any movement or commotion to tell me that it had alerted our captors to what we were doing.

I held a hand up, stopping Monica from speaking, as my head tilted. Nothing.

"Come here." I whispered.

She moved quickly over to me and I couldn't help it. I drew her into me and tilted her head up kissing her. Her fingers threaded through my hair, holding on tight, and kissing me back with everything that was in her. I could sense her trying to tell me everything we didn't have time for. I could feel that she didn't want to let go or stop. I was going to have to be strong enough for both of us.

Moving my large hands down her arms, pulling her back gently, she looked up at me, eyes watery and terrified.

"I'm gonna lift you through the window—"

"Trevor—" she started to argue.

"Hush," shaking my head, "I'm lifting you to the window and I'll push you through as far as I can." I continued. "You're gonna have to pull yourself out the rest of the way. I don't know what you're going into. Just run. Get coverage. Then run. Get as far away as fast as you can. When you think you've gotten far enough, run some more. Then get help."

"Trevor, I can't just leave you…"

"You can. You're going to. You have to."

She sobbed and my heart broke, knowing I probably wouldn't see her again. See Lacey or Lexi. But I'd be keeping my promise to Paul.

"Tell Lacey to fucking be good and cut you some slack. That's an order. Tell her I love her. Tell Lexi I love her too. It's going to be okay, Mon."

My head jerked to the side. *She fucking slapped me.*

"I'm not the mailman. You're going to tell them yourself." She was infuriated, belligerent and crying. Denial was in her eyes. I'd let her sit in it. But I'd said my peace. I knew when it came down to it, she'd tell them.

Leaning down I kissed her again, swiftly, before crouching and holding my hands in a cradle for her foot.

CHAPTER TWENTY EIGHT
MONICA

My head was spinning, disbelieving of the situation we were in. I placed my right foot into Trevor's hands and stared at him with what I knew was trepidation.

His green eyes never broke contact with mine as he stared at me one more time before he moved.

"You get through that window and run. Don't just stand there and look down or back at me. I'll be fine."

I just stared at him. Then nodded. There was no point in arguing.

"I love you..." I spoke softly. One more time.

He grinned. Despite the seriousness of the situation.

"I love you too, Mon. Now go." As he spoke he used all his strength to push off, giving me a sharp, sudden boost up to the window. My hands grasped at the sides, trembling. I only made it halfway out the frame and felt broken glass digging into me in places where it hadn't shattered.

I gritted my teeth, whimpering softly, as I felt Trevor's hands leave my foot. It was all on me now. Using what little upper body strength I had, I braced my palms on the concrete outside the window and pushed, barely squeezing through.

My frame was so much smaller than Trevor's. There was no way he could get out the window even if he could manage to get up to it. He'd known it. I blinked against the tears filling my eyes. I couldn't fall apart.

"Go, baby." Trevor urged, speaking quietly below me.

Groaning, I pulled myself up the rest of the way and stood shakily. I couldn't help it. I glanced back and down through the window to see Trevor glaring at me.

"Monica," he growled threateningly.

I spun on my heel and ran.

"What the hell was that?"

I froze and ducked behind a huge tree, knowing it was wide enough to hide my frame as I heard the gruff voice. It was one of the men who had been in the trees by the trailer. I held my breath, heart racing. Praying they wouldn't come around the side of the house to see the window.

Glancing around, it looked like the trees went on for some time. With it not being fully autumn yet, the summer growth provided foliage to better cover me. I tilted my head, thinking the area looked familiar. In my panic I hadn't paid attention to the outside of the house, when my body froze.

Peeking back around the trunk of the tree, I glanced back at the house and covered my mouth to prevent my audible gasp from being heard.

The old Paxton farmhouse.

The place where Becks had been taken.

The place where Paul had been killed.

Was I going to lose both of the loves of my life on the same cursed property?

It wasn't far from where Flinton had always parked his trailer and I was sure emergency services had responded quickly to that phone call. Especially with how panicked Lucas had sounded before I'd lost consciousness. I bit my lower lip, considering my options. I'd promised Trevor that I would get out and run.

But I was stubborn. I wasn't going to lose the two men I loved on the same property. I wasn't going to run. I was going to fight back.

Jogging carefully back to the side of the dilapidated house, I made sure to avoid the broken window I'd escaped from. My sides and lower stomach hurt and I was definitely bleeding from lacerations. Adrenaline was keeping me upright and the pain was minimal. Pretty positive it was shock and riding that high, I listened until I heard voices.

It sounded like Richard's men were on the front porch. Slowly creeping down the side of the house, I peered around the back to see if I could use anything to my advantage. One of them had left their vehicle back here. It was now or never. I knew they were at the front of the house and this may be the only chance I got.

Working my way over to the beat up pickup truck, I lifted the door handle, praying.

It was unlocked.

Opening the door slowly, I cringed as it creaked loudly and paused, tilting my head to listen. I didn't think anyone had heard it but I wasn't going to risk waiting. Sliding behind the wheel, cussing when I realized they hadn't left the keys in the ignition, I sighed, leaning over and opening the glove compartment.

Two handguns and some bullets greeted me, and I smiled.

"I guess those shooting lessons are going to pay off." I whispered, knowing Paul was always with me, sure that he was listening and watching. Paul would probably be somewhere between fiercely proud I was going to make a stand and absolutely livid I was risking it.

Checking both guns' chambers, I made sure they were loaded before exiting the vehicle. I didn't bother shutting the door, not wanting the men out front to hear me.

Tucking one gun in the back waistband of my leggings, I held the other carefully, moving back to the other side of the large farmhouse. There were two of them and one of me.

I had to make the first shot debilitating or fatal because the other one would be after me. I was trembling, trying to breathe in through my nose and out through my mouth to calm my body.

Peering around the side of the house I saw both men facing away from me. Both were grungy, with oily hair and ill-fitting clothing that had seen better days. They could pass for brothers, the only difference from the back being height. I looked closer, the one on the right was taller, broader.

I had a better chance if I took him out and was left with the smaller one. Gritting my teeth, I drew a calming breath in through my lungs. It was against everything in my nature to be violent. But these men had come for me. They had come for Trevor. They would keep coming and target my girls.

I knew they were attached to Larry and Clark in some way and those monsters had taken Paul away from me and nearly stolen my best friend.

Raising my arms, I sighted the bigger man, and fired.

I watched Monica disappear, knowing it went against her nature. Drawing deep calming breaths I listened for any noises. Anything to tell me they'd figured it out and were following her.

Hearing nothing after a few minutes, I sighed with relief and stared around at my surroundings. They'd be pissed when they figured out she was gone. Moving away from the light of the window, I walked back around the walls of the basement, searching for anything I could use to try to get out the door at the top of the stairs.

A gunshot rang out and I froze. Feeling like my blood was running cold in my veins. I pounded up the stairs, trying the door, knowing it was locked. Monica hadn't been gone long enough for that to not have involved her.

As another gun shot rang out, I yelled in frustration, slamming my shoulder into the door, I didn't give a fuck if it hurt. I needed to get out there.

"MONICA!" I yelled, feeling the most useless I ever had in my entire life. I heard one of the men yelling. It sounded like Mike. Then Monica's voice raised in fear and anger. I couldn't make out what they were saying. Just the yelling and chaos sending me into a range. Of all the things in this shitty house to hold strong, it would be this fucking basement door.

Another gunshot rang out and the voices stopped. Stepping to the top step again. I grabbed the railing and placed the opposite hand on the wall. Drawing my leg back I kicked the door as hard as I could. It cracked.

Turning, facing down the stairs, I braced myself again, kicking backward.

"FUCK!" I yelled, desperate.

I heard the door lock clicking and turned, ready to fight. What I didn't expect to see was Monica standing in front of me.

CHAPTER THIRTY

MONICA

I watched the bullet hit the back of the bigger man's head and he dropped immediately.

I'd just killed a man.

Nausea rolled through me, even as my arms straightened again, aiming quickly for the other man who was yelling and already turned toward me, infuriated.

"Fuck," I whispered to myself, eyes filling with tears, as I tried to blink them away. I fired again. Too soon. Not taking the time to aim properly.

"Crazy, psycho, bitch!" the man's voice yelled. "Fucking killed Chuck!"

Blinking I saw him coming at me still and I knew I'd missed. I took a step back too late as his hand circled my wrist, still holding the other handgun. I wasn't going out this way.

Reaching behind me, I drew the second gun, thankful Paul had given me lessons in shooting with either hand. I was awkward with my left and quite frankly sucked at aiming. But I had the advantage of surprise in my corner.

Drawing the other gun around, I aimed it at the man in front of me, even if it felt like he was breaking the wrist of my right hand, pointed the gun under his chin, and fired.

Everything exploded around me as he fell. I fell. Blood and other sorts of matter burst all over me. I gagged trying to keep hold of my bearings. I hit the ground on my hands and knees, staring into his wide, unseeing eyes, and felt tears dripping off my face.

Climbing to my feet, I picked up the gun, and sprinted towards the front door, sobbing.

I couldn't hold back my emotions anymore. I had just taken two men's lives. Pushing the door open I stumbled into the darkened house and hit a stack of cans, crying out as they fell.

Trevor's voice was screaming my name from the top of the stairs, but I couldn't answer. I was near hyperventilating. The smell of gasoline was strong and I was covered in something wet. I blinked looking at what I'd knocked over.

Gasoline canisters had been stacked right inside the front door and the fluid was creeping across the floor as I made my way to the basement door where Trevor was cursing. My hair was hanging in my face, my pony tail long gone and I'd lost my glasses after killing the second man. Everything was blurry and I was unsteady on my feet.

Unlocking the door, I swung it open, staring into Trevor's furious eyes. He was ready to fight.

"Monica?" he looked me up and down. "Fuck, fuck, fuck." he was up the last stair, his hands all over me searching for injuries. I probably looked like hell, covered in blood and gore.

I heard sirens in the distance, a car door slamming outside.

"WHAT THE FUCK?" a male voice screamed from outside.

Trevor tensed, grabbing my wrist, taking the gun from me.

"Richard," he whispered, pulling me deeper into the house.

My heart was pounding, my body begging for it to be over, to finally be able to shut down.

"Can you move?" Trevor whispered, backing me into the kitchen, taking me in. "Jesus, did you get shot?" his voice was breaking, his hands searching me again, even as we heard footsteps coming through the front door.

"No, it cuts from the windows." I whispered back, shakily.

"I heard gunshots."

"I killed them."

Trevor's green eyes shot up to mine, shocked.

"WHERE ARE YOU, CONNOR?" Richard's voice was moving through the house, coming towards the back, to the kitchen where we were located.

Moving towards a hallway at the back, Trevor shoved me through.

"I think this wraps back around to the living room." he whispered. "There were two entrances. We can come out from behind him. Get through the front door."

I nodded, trying to stop crying, trying to calm myself again.

Trevor squeezed my hand.

"It's almost over, just be brave a little longer for me, yeah?" he spoke softly, gently.

I tripped over the flooring going back into the living room. The door was feet from me. Escape. The sirens were louder.

"Not so fast, you dumb bitch." Richard's voice came from my left, and Trevor shot, firing the gun as he knocked me to the side out of the way.

Richard cursed and tackled him. I couldn't even tell if he'd been hit, and I was screaming at Trevor to shoot again. Standing shakily, I moved to the side, panicked, as Trevor got to his feet, Richard following, slower.

Trevor reared back, punching him in the jaw as hard as he could, and the floor where Richard fell gave under him causing some flooring to fall and shift.

"TREVOR!" I screamed, terrified the entire room would cave into the basement.

Trevor stepped back towards me and Richard lunged, grabbing his ankle. I scrambled to pick the gun up from where it had fallen and shot one more time, hitting Richard in the hand as he screamed and rolled to his back.

I watched in slow-motion as the floor gave way under him and he disappeared through it, into the basement, screaming for Trevor as he jumped, lunging to avoid going in after him.

Flames suddenly ignited, trailing all along the floor where the gasoline had spilled and spread. It was still running from the cans that had toppled over, some still stacked and full.

"Fuck!" Trevor said, bracing his hands on my waist. I cried out from the cuts, finally feeling some of the pain from crawling through the window, the gasoline that had poured on me stinging them.

"Go," Trevor ordered. "We need to get the fuck out of here. This place is going to blow."

Scrambling with him right after me, we cleared the front door as the rest of the floor caved in. I froze, staring at the gaping hole, as flames shot higher from the gasoline canisters. Trevor tackled me off the front porch and onto the lawn as everything went black.

Right before losing consciousness, all I saw were orange flames engulfing the entire Paxton farmhouse.

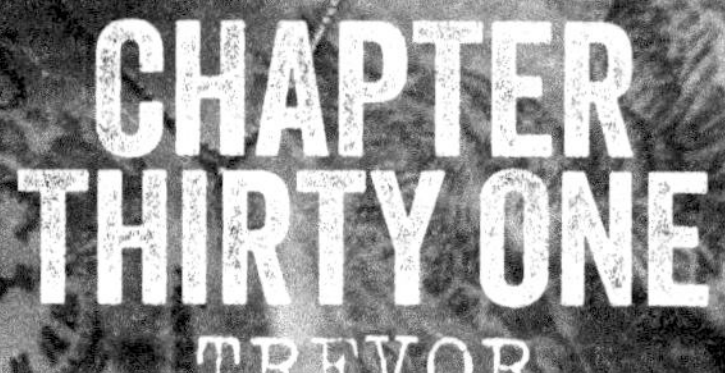

CHAPTER THIRTY ONE
TREVOR

I felt the hear of the blast behind me as I curled myself over Monica, protecting her. Feeling her body still underneath me, I panicked, getting on my hands and knees.

Staring down at her unconscious form I yelled, "Monica!" My hands, covered in dirt, shoved her hair off her face, her ponytail long gone. She was too still. I moved, shoving the sweatshirt she was wearing up and off along with the shirt under it. Both were sodden with gasoline and blood and I wasn't positive she hadn't been shot and wasn't just blocking it out.

"Baby, come on." My voice was breaking, even as I heard tires spinning on the gravel, sirens blaring. Help had arrived, but at what cost?

Her lower stomach and sides were bleeding badly, lacerations from the broken glass in the window. I cursed, yanking my own shirt off to lay across them and applied pressure.

"Fuck. What the fuck happened?" I heard Lucas' voice even

as he hit his knees beside me.

"Richard, Mike, and Chuck." I rattled off. "They're all dead. Jackson is dead. Monica's hurt." all my training was out the window. I couldn't even focus on giving details. Someone grabbed my arm to pull me back and I swung.

"Jesus. Dude. Stop. They need to help." Nick's voice broke through my terror. He stood, pulling me with him, to watch as EMTs swarmed the woman I loved.

"Is she okay?" I demanded, leaning over them, begging them to tell me she was fine.

"So far vitals are good. We're going to take her into the hospital. She's got trauma and blood loss. We have a full vehicle, do you have a ride?" the female paramedic asked.

"I'm riding with her." I argued.

"You can't do that right now and you're holding us up." the woman stated firmly.

"I've got him. We're right behind you." Lucas' voice broke through my anger and frustration.

"Nick?"

"I've got the scene." Nick affirmed, even as the ambulance sped off and I headed towards Lucas' truck.

"Come on." I ordered, as Lucas climbed in, starting the truck and slamming it into gear to follow.

"I've got a sweatshirt or something you can put on in the back." he stated gruffly, and I blinked down at myself, tattooed chest bare. Because my shirt was stopping Monica's bleeding.

Monica. Who was hurt.

In an ambulance without me.

"FUCK." I growled, hitting the console.

"HEY!" Lucas yelled, keeping his eyes on the road, sparing

me half a glance. "It won't help her if you fall apart. Get a fucking shirt on and get ready to be there for her." he ordered.

I glared at him, ready to fight, Even as he glanced at me again.

"Don't make me knock some fucking sense into you, asshole." he stated firmly.

Shaking my head, I knew he was right. I turned searching through the bags in the back before pulling out a Reading Police Department shirt and pulling it over my head.

"Remind me to get a picture of that for Monica when she wakes up." he grumbled, almost laughing.

I just glared at him.

"She's going to be fine, man. She's been through trauma and lost blood. They'll get her fixed up. She's stronger than she looks."

I just looked out the window as we entered the town. We sped through the streets to the hospital where they'd taken Monica.

Lucas' vehicle screeched to a stop behind the ambulance and we jumped out hitting the emergency entrance just as they took Monica past the doors to the back.

"Officer Marshall!" a chipper voice spoke, even as I made to follow where they'd disappeared.

"Not now," Lucas' voice was rough, more rude than he'd usually be.

"Um…. weren't you on your way to labor and delivery?" the female voice spoke more hesitantly now.

I froze, spinning to look towards Lucas who had turned into a living statue.

"Um…Officer Marshall?" The nurse looked between Lucas and I worriedly.

"Fuck," I muttered, stepping up to my friend. Snapping my

fingers in front of his face, "Dude!" I spoke harshly. "Snap the fuck out of it."

He blinked, coming back into focus.

"Labor and delivery? Where? Where is she?"

The nurse stared at both of us, eyes huge, "Um…third floor, room three-eighty-nine."

I watched Lucas take off, bypassing the elevators and hitting the stairwell, the door slamming behind him.

I prayed Becks was okay and he wasn't walking into his own nightmare, even as I turned and went through the doors to get to Monica.

Walking down the chaotic hallway, I glanced into each room looking for Monica when a nurse poked her head out of a room two doors down.

"Mr. Connor?" she questioned, looking at me.

"That's me." I walked the last few steps to her hurriedly.

Smiling softly, she spoke, "She's okay and awake. She's asking for you, rather furiously actually," her sentence ended with a soft laugh.

"I said, I'm fine!" Monica's voice came out of the room, seemingly frustrated. "Where's Trevor? Is he okay?"

"Mrs. Rogers, he is fine. He rode behind the ambulance with a police officer…" the young, male doctor's voice cut off, exasperated as he spotted me coming inside the room. "Are you Trevor?" he asked, pleadingly.

My eyes found Monica's and she stopped struggling, leaning back against the stretcher they had her on, her eyes filling with tears.

"I'm Trevor," I confirmed, walking to her bedside and grabbing hold of her hand. "Let them do what they need to," my voice came out soft, ordering her gently. "You lost a lot of blood and probably have a concussion."

"You're okay?" she asked.

"I'm fine," I assured her, leaning down and kissing her forehead. "You're far worse off than I am."

"How do we know you don't have a concussion?" she asked. "They knocked you out."

I glowered down at her, even as the doctor's voice broke in.

"We're gonna probably want to check that out too." he began.

I looked up, something in my eyes cutting him off.

"After we take care of you first." he finished, looking back down at Monica.

CHAPTER THIRTY TWO
MONICA

I gasped softly as the nurse finished dabbing the stitches. Twenty-eight spread out across my lower abdomen. A tetanus shot and concussion later, I was ready to flee this room. The entire damn hospital. I hated them.

"Remember what the doctor said," the nurse spoke softly, finishing the bandaging. "You have a concussion. The only reason we're letting you go is because Mr. Connor has some paramedic training with him being a firefighter."

"I know," I said, swinging my legs off. "I'm sorry. I just hate hospitals."

"We get that a lot around here. I don't take offense," she laughed.

I heard Trevor's voice in the hallway. The jerk hadn't even had to get on a stretcher. They'd just taken him to another room for a quick concussion assessment. How unfair was that?

"Thanks, Dr. Halmer," he said calmly in that stupid beautiful voice.

"You two just take care of each other. I'll wanna see her in about a week to remove the stitches, although she'll probably talk you into doing it."

Trevor laughed as I came to the room's doorway, watching him shake the young doctor's hand. I tugged the slightly snug shirt down that the hospital had found for me to go home in.

"I'm ready to get out of here." I spoke as he turned to face me.

"Let me get a wheelchair, Jesus." he spoke, stepping over to me worriedly.

"Trevor. I'm fine. Other than stitches and a hell of a headache, I'm fine." I pushed his chest gently.

Huffing out a breath, blowing his bangs off his forehead, he glowered down at me.

"Okay. Don't get mad…"

"That's never a good way to start a sentence." I said, interjecting, feeling nervous suddenly.

"I just didn't want you shooting up off the bed before the doctors and nurses were done with you." he argued, gently. "But, when Lucas and I came in, a nurse stopped us because she thought I was bringing Lucas to the hospital."

"Was he hurt?" I blurted out, worriedly.

"No…" Trevor's voice trailed off. "They thought he was here for Becks…"

"WHAT?" I practically yelled. "What's wrong with Becks?"

"I don't know, I just know she's up in labor and delivery."

"Well, I'm not leaving until I know she's okay." I spoke, walking outside the emergency room doors and over to the elevator doors, pushing the button. I fought off a sick feeling at the last time I'd been here, when Becks had been hurt and Paul had been killed. I drew in a shaky breath as Trevor's arm came around my shoulders pulling me tight against his body, like he was reading my mind.

"I'm right here, Mon," he whispered.

"I know," I spoke softly, leaning against him. "I just hate it here."

He squeezed me gently as we entered the elevator, pressing the floor for labor and delivery. I watched the number three light up as it carried us up, my stomach dropping like it always did in these damn things.

"Becks will be okay" Trevor continued speaking as the doors opened. "Her and the baby will be fine."

I nodded, leading him out of the elevator and heading towards the nurses' station.

"Can we help you?" The male nurse looked at us.

"We're here for Rebecca Marshall." I spoke, my voice shaky.

"You're the sister!" he exclaimed, nodding. "Monica?"

I breathed a sigh of relief that Lucas and Becks had put me down as family.

"Right. And this is my husband, Trevor." I said, nodding.

"Great. I'll come around to open the door and bring the visitor's badges. You'll need to wear them the entire time you're on this floor and check out when you leave. We like to keep our babies and mommies safe." he said, disappearing out the back of the station.

"Husband?" Trevor's voice was low as I spun to face him.

"I know, I'm sorry…"

Then his lips were crashing down on mine, fingers threading through my hair that had long since come down from my ponytail, angling my head to kiss my deeper.

"Oh….ahem…"

I pulled back, blushing, as Trevor's darkened green eyes stared down at me.

"Sorry to interrupt," the nurse continued.

"It's fine. Sorry about that," Trevor said, still looking at me, "Newlyweds." he shrugged then, breaking eye contact and smiling at the nurse.

I snorted before I could stop myself, covering my mouth as I laughed.

"You two are adorable. Oh my God." said the nurse. "Sign me up for a man in uniform." he joked, opening the door wider with his hip as we stepped through.

Trevor choked, blushing, as I threw my head back and laughed loudly.

"They are a different breed." I acknowledged.

Making sure the door was securely locked behind him, the nurse moved in front of us, walking quickly.

"I'm Zachary, preferably Zach," he spoke, glancing back over his shoulder. "Mrs. Marshall is currently in the delivery room, this is our waiting room. Help yourselves to the drinks or snacks or there are vending machines down the hall, bathroom across from them. We'll keep you updated as we can." he spoke, gesturing to the cozy waiting room lined with plastic chairs and couches.

"Delivery room?" I asked, worriedly. "It's too early…" I trailed off.

Zach reached out, patting my shoulder understandingly.

"It is," he agreed. "But she's in the best place she can be for her and the baby now. Plus, her own tall-dark-and-handsome came sprinting in here to be with her a few hours ago."

My hands covered my face, trying to hold back my tears,

as I heard Trevor wrapping up the conversation with him. He guided me over to the couch to sit and I grimaced as I sat down, the stitches pulling slightly.

"I know it's no use trying to talk you into going home—"

"You're right, it's not." I interjected.

Trevor quirked an eyebrow, "I am going to get you something to drink…not coffee, water first." He said sensing my argument. "And something small to eat. There's nothing we can do right now. You're going to eat and drink something."

I crossed my arms. I'd missed this. Someone taking care of me. I still wasn't used to it being him again. Even though we'd been living together for a few months. Paul had always been the one to do it, combatting my stubbornness.

"Ok." I conceded. "Are the girls okay? Still at Nan's?" I asked. I was worried about Lacey. Telling her about her friend being gone. Losing someone so close to having lost Paul. My eyes teared up thinking about it and a tear slipped down my cheek. Trevor crouched in front of me, brushing it away with his thumb.

"They're fine. Last I checked they were watching some teen flick with Nan and she had a pallet all made up on the floor for a sleepover. She's living her best life right now and so are they. I assured them you are fine and I am fine. They're just worried about Becks and the baby too. I didn't say anything to Lacey or the other two about Jackson. We'll cross that bridge when we get to it. Together."

I nodded, sobbing softly, even as he pulled me into his arms. It's like he'd read my whole mind and handled everything. The adrenaline and chaos of the evening was wearing off and I hurt more than I was letting on. I was scared once again that I would lose my best friend and the sweet little baby she couldn't carry to term. I clutched Trevor tighter against me, holding on.

"So…husband, huh?" he asked softly, chuckling.

I jerked back, turning red. "I'm sorry about that. I just wanted you with me, and if they were only letting family—"

His lips tipped up in a grin.

"I'm not sorry," he teased. "I like the way that sounded. My husband." his thumb trailed over my lower lip gently. "We'll have to see about making that official." his voice lowered, going quieter, even as my breath caught in my throat. "I'm gonna go get your snack. Water or juice?" he asked, standing.

My mind was whirling with what he'd just said.

"Juice," I requested, gaping at him.

"Got it," he said, turning and exiting the waiting room, leaving me alone.

CHAPTER THIRTY THREE
TREVOR

"I can't believe they're all dead…" I spoke softly, staring into the vending machine's window. Monica would want something salty and then sweet. I had already gotten her some grape juice and a bottle of water. I'd thought about ordering a pizza, but I was pushing it with getting her to eat a couple snacks already. She was under a lot of stress and worried. I was barely holding on myself. Still seeing her bloodied and beat up when I'd opened that basement door.

"It's over." spoke Nick, gruffly. "The old farmhouse is gone. We let it burn to the ground actually. After everything that's happened there." his voice trailed off.

"Nick, you know this isn't your fault." I said, selecting a chocolate bar to go with the peanuts I'd gotten Monica. "There was nothing any of us could've done to prevent what happened to Jackson."

"I know," his voice was rough, terse. "I just feel like I was responsible for him, like I let him down somehow. He knew not to go there alone."

I shook my head, even though he couldn't see me.

"He'd dealt with a lifetime of abuse, man." I said softly. "I know Jackson wouldn't want you to feel this way, carry this."

"Alright. Anything from Lucas?" Nick's voice was even more short with me, changing the subject. I'd have to worry about him, the effect this was going to have on him, later.

"Nothing. Last I heard she was in delivery," I updated him, walking back down the hallway.

"Too fucking early." he muttered.

"Yep. I'll keep you updated as I know something." I said, speeding up as I heard voices in the waiting room.

Rounding the corner, placing my phone back in my pocket, I saw Lucas standing with his back to me. His hair was standing on end, like he'd been running his fingers through it distractedly.

"They're okay though…" he trailed off, as I walked around him. Monica had her hands covering her mouth, tears rolling down her face, even as the big man pulled her into a hug.

"I'm so fucking glad you're okay," he added. "Both of you."

Monica just continued to cry against his chest, hugging him back, as he reached out a hand to me.

I grasped it, raising an eyebrow questioningly.

"Baby is here and fine." he explained, as Monica stepped back, wiping her tears and I placed an arm around her. "He's tiny. So fucking small. He's having some trouble breathing. They want to monitor him." his voice broke.

"Becks was apparently seven centimeters when Lucas got up here." Monica picked up, "and letting everyone in the room know that the baby was staying put until her husband got here." she laughed tearfully. "She said and I quote, 'I'm not fucking doing this alone again' and had them all terrified."

Lucas chuckled, running a tattooed hand through his hair again.

"She was in battle mode, man" his gray eyes met mine. "I've never quite seen her like that. The whole part of the labor I caught and delivery was…" he shook his head.

"I know, man. It's incredible what these women can do." I agreed with him.

Monica laughed, shaking her head at my side. "It doesn't feel fucking magical." she murmured.

"They want to keep her for observation overnight. But she's fine. Becks did beautiful. They're getting her cleaned up and then you all can come back. She demanded the bathroom and a shower and ordered me to go with the baby. She swore me to secrecy."

"Ugh…I'm dying to meet my nephew!" groaned Monica.

"Patience," I soothed, smiling down at her.

Lucas laughed. "Sorry. I'd rather face your anger than my extremely hormonal wife's."

"I'll let it slide this time." Monica returned.

"I'm gonna go check on baby boy and mama," Lucas said, nearly slipping. "I'll come get you when Becks is ready."

"Alright, brother. Congratulations." I said.

"Tell Becks we love her," added Monica.

"Will do, you two." Lucas turned, leaving the room.

Monica sighed, shaking her head. "I cannot believe the baby is here." she said, looking at me.

"They'll be fine." I assured her. "He is in the best place for them and it sounds like other than being early, and needing some time to catch up, everything else went perfectly."

She nodded, wrapping her arms around my waist, cuddling into me.

"I checked in on the girls. They're asleep, and Nan was headed to bed. She said to just leave them there until we get some rest tomorrow. She'll probably kick all our asses if Lucas didn't call her before he told us anything."

Monica chuckled, then sat down groaning.

"You're in more pain than you're letting on." I accused her.

"Alright. Maybe I am." she admitted, grabbing the peanuts and juice from me.

"Trevor…"

Lucas' voice came through like it was in a tunnel and I blinked my eyes open slowly. My back and neck ached from the position I'd fallen asleep in on the hard plastic sofa. Glancing down I saw Monica was still asleep, laid out, head on my lap.

My eyes met Lucas' and I spoke quietly.

"Everything okay?"

He nodded, glancing down at Monica himself.

"Becks is ready to see you all if you want." he spoke in a whisper, "I just didn't know if you wanted to wake Monica up just yet or…"

"She'll put us both on another floor of this hospital if we don't." I joked.

"Mon," I spoke softly, running my hand down her arm.

She groaned, her face twisting in pain and I felt a rush of irritation that she'd talked me into letting her stay here when she was in so much pain. There hadn't been any compromise with her.

Until she set her own eyes on her best friend, we weren't leaving.

"What," her voice grumped, raspy with sleep.

"Becks is ready to see you," Lucas spoke, standing up to his full height again.

Monica jerked upright, grimacing in pain, her hand going to her abdomen.

"Jesus. Would you take it slow, woman?" I growled.

"Let's go," she ignored me, standing up gingerly, ready to follow the tall cop.

Going down the quiet hallway of the labor and delivery unit, Lucas came to Becks' door. Knocking and opening it gently, we entered the room to see the new mother laying in her bed, glowing.

Becks' eyes grew big, taking in how her friend was moving, and she shot me a concerned look.

"Monica, you shouldn't have stayed when you were this hurt." she scolded, even as the two women hugged like they'd been apart for a decade. "I'm so glad you're okay." Becks continued, tearfully.

"We're fine." I assured Becks, "Monica is banged up and needs to heal but there was no convincing her to go home when you were here." I added.

"I had to make sure you were okay too." spoke Monica, standing and looking down at Becks, tearful herself. "Are you okay? How's the baby?"

Becks wiped the tears off her face, still holding Monica's hand. She met Lucas' eyes and smiled.

"He's perfect."

Monica nearly shrieked excitedly as Becks nodded and Lucas and I laughed. I shook my friend's hand.

"Congratulations, you two." I said, elated for them.

"His lungs just need to grow a little more. He needs some extra help." Becks said, worriedly.

"They said he'd be fine, hon." spoke Lucas, moving to her other side. "He'll be in the NICU for a while. Then we're taking our son home." his hand rubbed her shoulder softly.

"What's his name?" asked Monica.

"You tell them." said Becks, reaching up and placing her hand over Lucas'.

The gruff, stoic man cleared his throat, and I was surprised to hear his voice crack as he spoke.

"We named him William so we could call him Will, like we did my grandpa Willard."

"That's beautiful!" exclaimed Monica, squeezing Becks' hand.

"But his middle name is Paul." Lucas' gray eyes met mine, then Monica's as I heard her let out a soft sob. I moved up to her, placing my arm around her shoulders to draw her into me tight.

"William Paul," Monica echoed, staring at her friend with tears running down her face. Becks' was crying now too, and I even had to run my hands over my eyes.

"Paul would've been…" Monica's voice trailed off, shaking her head.

"I know," whispered Becks.

CHAPTER THIRTY FOUR

MONICA

One Month Later

"Would you slow down?"

Trevor griped at me as I finished placing the cake on the table. I turned and glared at him.

"Excuse me. It's not everyday that your best friend gets to bring her son home from the hospital."

"I just want you to be careful." he interjected, staring at me with those green eyes.

"I know," I spoke softer, knowing he was still scared of how hurt I'd been and how much we'd been through this year. "But, I'm fine. All healed. If anything, doing this is helping me work through things. Our godson is coming home today!" fully aware that I was squealing.

Lacey walked into Becks and Lucas' kitchen, crossing her arms and staring at us.

"Hey, sweetie." Trevor wrapped a large, tattooed arm around her and pulled our daughter close. She was struggling with Jackson's death and the trauma that came along with it. We all were. It was so hard to see someone who had just started out in their life get it cut so short and so quick. Combined with it being during her senior year and after losing Paul? We'd decided to put her into therapy. Both of us were shocked when she'd readily agreed. Becks had referred us to a therapist in the same clinic as the one she went to and it was going well although slow.

The doorbell rang and I heard Lexi and Nat running to answer it. Walking out to stand behind them I smiled at Nick and Caroline. My eyebrow quirked taking in their mannerisms, awkward and tense.

"Hey, guys. I'm so glad you two could come. Caroline, I told you that you didn't have to bring anything!" I exclaimed.

"It's just a lasagna they can eat tonight, or freeze for later, some cupcakes, and cookies. We'll just say it's my gift."

"She wouldn't let me help her up with them." Nick practically growled, pushing past me and going into the house.

The poor man was taking Jackson's death horribly, shouldering the blame like he'd been his son to take care of. I knew Lucas and Trevor had been trying to talk to him, keep him company as much as they could. But Nick, although being all of our friend, had always been a bit of a mystery to us.

I looked back at Caroline, watching her blue eyes follow Nick disappear into the kitchen. Lacey and Trevor's voices greeting him.

"Girls, why don't you take the stuff into the kitchen for Caroline?" I asked the two younger girls.

Once they'd gone on their way with the items I really gave the other woman a once-over. She looked like she was a mess. More tired than usual and her smile wasn't making her blue eyes light up.

"Are you okay?" I asked, worriedly.

Caroline shook her head, her blonde ponytail bouncing with the movement.

"Oh, I'm fine. Just a little tired." she spoke, stepping forward and hugging me. "When will Lucas and Becks be here?"

I glanced down at my smart watch.

"Any minute actually." I grabbed her arm pulling her inside, forgetting to give her the third degree. That could come later. I'd have Becks as back up for it.

Caroline laughed as I pulled her into the living room, the men and girls coming in. I watched Trevor observe Nick glowering at Caroline and he looked at me questioningly. All I could do was shrug. Something was definitely going on there. Trevor glanced out the window when we heard a loud engine.

"They're here," he proclaimed. Nat took off out of the room, flying through the front door. When Lexi made to follow, I grabbed her wrist.

"Give them a minute." I told her, pulling my tiny redhead to me.

I heard Lucas greeting Nat and Becks' softer voice.

"Hey, Peanut!"

"Monica didn't go overboard did she?"

Trevor stared pointedly at me upon hearing Becks' statement and I made an effort to pretend like I didn't see him. Then they were coming through the front door.

"Welcome home!" I proclaimed, alongside Caroline.

Becks' laughed, her arm slung around Nat's shoulders as Lucas followed with the baby carrier.

"Monica!" my friend squealed. "I didn't expect a whole party."

"You would've done the same for me." I argued. "Give me

my godson."

Lucas set the baby carrier on the coffee table and turned it to face the room. The chubby little boy looked at all of us stoically before gurgling a coo. My heart melted.

"Oh, he's beautiful!!" exclaimed Caroline, coming forward, clutching her hands under her chin. "You all make beautiful babies." she added.

"I did well, didn't I?" bragged Lucas as Becks swatted him, blushing.

"You caveman," she joked.

Trevor walked over, undoing the seat belt in the carrier and picked Will up, holding him against his chest. Massive tattooed arms careful around the baby. My stomach did a flip seeing him like that. We were far past the baby stage, but I could admire him holding my friends' baby. It did things to me. Trevor smirked at me like he knew exactly what I was thinking.

"I had called dibs," I pouted, glaring at him playfully.

"I got there first."

"We can take turns," assured Becks, giggling at us.

Later after dinner, the girls were upstairs watching a movie while the men sat on the patio. Caroline, Becks, and I were in her library Lucas' had built last Christmas. Our new friend sat in the cushy recliner holding Will on her chest, cooing at him while we talked.

"Becks, he is seriously perfect." she said again softly.

"Thanks," said Becks. "I think so too but I'm pretty biased. I never thought I'd be a mother again at forty."

"Better you than me," I said, crossing my legs in the seat I'd perched on.

"How's Nick doing?" asked Becks softly.

I watched Caroline's eyes darken at the man's name, staring down at Will.

"He's still beating himself up over Jackson. He knows it wasn't his fault, but he does this. He's always been the most stoic and quiet out of all the men. Trevor is trying to not let him be alone with his thoughts too much."

Becks nodded, "Has he said anything to you, Caroline?"

Carolines eyes jerked up to Becks.

"What? No! Why?" she asked.

"Lucas had just said Nick seemed to be going into the cafe more and thought you all may be getting to know one another." said Becks, unsure now.

"Nope. Nope, nothings going on."

Becks' dark eyes met mine and she raised her eyebrows. There was something going on there and we'd have to get it out of one of them eventually.

A tapping on the door and its opening had us looking towards it to see the man in question frozen in the doorway, staring at Caroline holding a baby. After a long awkward pause, Becks spoke.

"Nick?"

Jerking his head, he glanced over at her.

"I've gotta go to the station. I just wanted to say bye and congratulations again." spinning on his heel, he turned and left before anyone could respond.

Caroline stood walking the baby over to Becks and placing him in his mother's arms.

"I've actually gotta go too. I told Mom I'd help her with some baking before tomorrow." then she was gone in a blonde blur.

"What the fuck was that?" asked Becks, looking at me as the door shut behind our friends.

"Hell if I know?!" I answered.

"Do you think they're sleeping together?"

"BECKS!"

"You were thinking it."

CHAPTER THIRTY FIVE

TREVOR

"So, Lexi and Lacey. You go get Becks, the baby, and your mom from the library." I said, trying to remain calm. I'd spoken to Lucas and Becks about this a couple of weeks ago and they were fine with it. I had both Lacey and Lexi's permissions too.

As my two girls left, Nat spoke, staring at me worriedly.

"Uncle Trevor, you don't look so good."

Lucas barked out a laugh.

"You've been married before, man. To her, actually," he said, shaking his head.

"I know. This is just different." I defended myself and my nerves. We'd set candles around the living room and when we heard the back door open again, Nat and Lucas disappeared to the kitchen.

"What are you all up to?"

Monica's voice was suspicious.

"Nothing," came Becks' quieter voice.

"I think Trevor got a call from the station." answered Lucas' deeper voice. "He just wanted to let you know and I'll take you guys home."

I heard Monica sigh and start towards the living room, so I went ahead and got down on one knee, opening the velvet box and looking up as she entered.

She gasped when she turned the corner and saw me, her eyes filling with tears.

"Trevor Connor…" she spoke softly.

"Come here," I nearly begged. I watched the love of my life come towards me, wearing her leggings and oversized sweatshirt. Smiling at her signature messy bun. I wouldn't have her any other way and after everything we'd been through to get here, we could get married wearing the clothes on our backs, and I'd be elated.

"What are you doing?" she whispered, still disbelieving as I grabbed her hand.

"I didn't want that male nurse to find out you lied to him," I began as she laughed, throwing her head back.

"Monica," I continued, "I love you more than anything else on this Earth, outside of our daughters," I got serious now, her eyes meeting mine, "I know fourteen years ago, I fucked up. I was a kid. Hell we both were. That's no excuse, but I ruined the best thing that ever happened to me."

"Trevor," she whispered.

"Hush. You found someone that I will be eternally grateful to, that took care of you and our daughter. You both gave me another little girl to love like my own. You both believed in me and I in no way expect to replace him in their lives or yours. But, if you'd give me the chance to show you what it always should've been like with us, I promise I'll make you the happiest woman alive and take care of you, and those girls forever. Will you marry me…again?"

Monica's brown eyes were shining through her tears in the living room as her head bobbed in a nod before she managed to say yes.

I slid the ring onto her finger, pushing it down to rest alongside the sapphire one Paul had designed for Lucas and Becks to give her last Christmas that she wore on her middle finger. The oval diamond shone pink up at me beside it.

"Pink?" she asked, wiping her eyes behind her glasses.

"It's your favorite color," I said, standing up to tower over her. Taking her face in my tattooed hands I leaned down and kissed her deeply while the room behind her filled with our loved ones.

The teenagers were so excited they were jumping around like little kids, Becks was crying and congratulating us when I pulled back, and Lucas shook my hand, scooping Monica into a huge hug.

Lacey had her nose twisted up, although she was grinning.

"Did you all have to make out like that?" she asked.

"That wasn't making out." I replied. "If you want I can give a demonstration…"

"Ew no!" she shrieked as the adults laughed.

"I'm so happy for you all," said Becks, patting Will's back as he laid against her chest. "Now I get to help plan your wedding like you did mine."

I felt myself pale again as the two women shrieked and started talking, Lucas laughed at the look on my face.

"I just thought we'd do something small and intimate." I said, causing both women to freeze and stare at me appalled.

"You're cute," said Becks, grabbing Monica's hand to pull her to the kitchen.

"Fuck," I muttered as Lucas watched gleefully.

CHAPTER THIRTY SIX
CAROLINE

"You know you're going to have to talk to me eventually right?" I asked, storming after Nick around the side of the house. "Other than to just be a bossy asshole."

I watched his body tense, turning slowly to face me, his brown eyes flashing with anger and something else. I came toe-to-toe with him, crossing my arms and craning my neck to stare.

"You really wanna do this here?" he practically growled, glaring down at me. I took him in, towering over me, tattoos covering him from the neck down. Brown hair longer on top and threaded heavily with gray, along with his short beard.

Nick Larson was a forty-four year old man. Fifteen years my senior. The mysterious bachelor of the town that nobody knew.

A month ago he'd come into the cafe when we were closed and I'd forgotten to lock the door. Dazed and a mess from the shift he'd just finished. I hadn't turned him away. I'd gotten him some cookies and hot tea. I'd been worried about the look in his eyes.

He'd almost seemed to stare vacantly through me. When he'd started to leave, I'd come around the corner and given him a hug without even thinking. I'd always had a thing for older men. When he'd come in with Lucas, Trevor, and the guys, I'd admired him from afar.

I hadn't expected him to lose control that night. After the hug we'd pulled back and I'd been pinned under his stare.

The next thing I'd known we were kissing. It was unlike any other encounter I'd ever had. The way he'd taken control yet ensured consent. The way he'd reached over and locked the cafe's door and then taken me.

I didn't regret it.

But he seemed to.

"Caroline," he said, rubbing his hand over his face, my eyes drank in the tattoos there hungrily. I loved every bit of him. I had since I'd gotten back into town and I'd first set eyes on him. "We can't do this. It was a one time thing. I don't do relationships. It's not you. I've always been this way."

Scowling up at him I asked, "So, what happened that night? Everything that clicked with us was just a one off?" I whispered.

Something in his eyes softened before he threw his guard back up.

"You're fifteen years younger than me, Caroline. This can't happen." he turned and stomped off to his police vehicle, slamming the door and peeling out.

I stood watching his taillights turn at the end of the street.

If Nick Larson didn't want me, if Nick Larson was the same as every other male in my life, then I'd just raise this baby alone.

CHAPTER THIRTY SEVEN

NICK

I pulled over once I left Lucas and Becks' street. Into another quiet neighborhood and slammed my hands against the steering wheel. That fucking woman. This is why I only slept with women that I never saw again.

I couldn't get her blonde hair and blue eyes out of my mind.

The taste of her mouth.

The sound of her cries.

The perfection of her submission.

Caroline Foster had come back to town and thrown me for a loop. I'd felt her eyes on me since she'd gotten back. I'd been flirtatious.

I don't even know how I'd ended up at the cafe after finishing my shift the night Jackson had died. I was a mess and feeling guilty as hell.

There she fucking was with her cookies and hot tea. Then coming around and pressing that body up against me.

The next thing I'd known I had the door locked and her on the counter in the back. She didn't shy away from my roughness, my need for control. I wouldn't call myself a Dom. But I liked calling the shots.

I liked giving pleasure to such an extreme that women were sobbing and nearly blacking out by the time I was done with them.

She'd broken so beautifully for me.

I growled, slamming my head into the headrest and hitting my steering wheel again.

It couldn't happen again.

Who cares if she had been perfect?

If she'd consented and followed my every demand?

If she'd been the perfection I'd been looking for my entire life, but never deserved.

It couldn't happen.

She was fifteen years younger than me.

She deserved someone her own age. Someone she could have children with and who could be a good father. I couldn't even take care of a nineteen-year-old that wasn't my child.

I needed to move on.

CHAPTER THIRTY EIGHT

MONICA

Three Months Later

"This is ridiculous," I said, staring at myself in the mirror. "I have been married twice. People are going to talk. Maybe we should've just done something small."

Becks came up behind me, wearing a soft pink bridesmaid's dress, hair in a casual updo with curls framing her face.

"Monica," she spoke, softly. "You deserve this. Fuck what everyone else thinks."

I snorted, laughing at her language, "You're in a church."

"So, you know I'm serious then."

"Fine," I said, adjusting the skirt of the mermaid style wedding dress I'd chosen. "Are the girls ready to give me away?"

"They're at the back of the church waiting," she assured me.

Even if we were doing this up right, with an actual wedding, we hadn't invited a lot of people. Just my parents and Caroline Foster. She probably wouldn't show up though, having gone back to the city suddenly three months ago.

Lucas, Nick, and Will were standing up with Trevor. Will looked adorable in his little infant tux.

"Lucas was doing something in that tux holding that baby" Becks wiggled her eyebrows at me.

I laughed again. "Men with babies are something else," I said, thinking about the moments Trevor had held the tiny baby boy.

"Paul would be happy for you," my friend spoke softly, hitting the exact reason I was so nervous right now.

"Yeah?" I asked my brown eyes meeting hers in the mirror.

"Definitely." she continued to assure me. "Now, let's go get you married."

CHAPTER THIRTY NINE

TREVOR

Monica was beautiful.

As I watched her coming down the aisle with Lexi and Lacey on either side of her, I found myself tearing up. Lacey caught my eye and shook her head at me, rolling her eyes.

I found myself winking at my oldest daughter, relieved she was doing better after several months in therapy. Lexi had been pretty quiet about all of this, which we expected. We knew her father was on her mind even though she was happy for her mother and I. Even the younger redhead was smiling at me though and I winked at her too.

Will was cooing behind me, held by Lucas, and I turned glancing over my shoulder at them both. Lucas shrugged apologetically but we weren't bothered. Monica and I loved that little man like he was our own son.

Becks was giggling at her son's noises across the altar from me and the preacher was sending her a stern look even as Nat was shushing her own mother.

Looking a little further behind Lucas, I met Nick's brown eyes. He looked like a fish out of water in his tux and I couldn't help chuckling at him even as his eyes narrowed at me.

"I'll kick your ass," he mouthed.

The ceremony was short and sweet. Everything Monica wanted, and I didn't deserve, getting to claim her as my own for the rest of our lives.

When the preacher announced us as Mr. and Mrs. Trevor Connor I dipped her back and kissed her thoroughly. My bride was beautifully breathless when I stood her back up and we walked back down the aisle to start the rest of our lives.

CHAPTER FORTY
CAROLINE

I heard the church bells pinging down the street as I pulled into the parking spot in front of my parent's cafe.

I was back. Four months pregnant and absolutely terrified. I never had wanted to return to this town and been content to stay gone forever. Nick didn't want me. No one but my parents knew I was pregnant.

I'd ended up with a different company in the city the last three months, but when problems from the other company I'd worked for followed me there, I'd run again. This was the only other place I had.

My hand rested on the soft swell of my stomach. I wasn't majorly showing yet, but with my height and being tiny, it would be sooner rather than later. I was having a very difficult pregnancy and the problems I'd faced hadn't made it any easier.

I closed my eyes against the memories that were bombarding me. How was I to know that my new boss was so close to my old one?

Stepping out of my car, I stared down the street where people were exiting the church until I saw a familiar form.

Almost like something inside me called to him, his eyes jerked up meeting mine immediately. Widening slightly at the sight of me.

I tried to stop my heart from beating so quickly.

He doesn't want you, Caroline.

I wish I'd just told him and never left. He was going to be furious if I told him now. Especially if he ever found out what had happened to me while I'd been carrying his baby.

CHAPTER FORTY ONE

NICK

My eyes stayed on the blonde woman standing down the street, even as she turned to go into the cafe behind her. Caroline Foster was back in town. Something primal rushed through me to stomp down there and yank her into my vehicle. Take her to my house and demand to know why she'd left me.

But you know why she left you, dickhead.

I shook my head, even as a hand slapped down on my shoulder.

"You okay, man?" Lucas asked as I turned to face him.

"I'm good," I answered, stiffly. I slid my hands into my pockets as we watched Trevor and Monica climb into their vehicle. They were leaving immediately for a short honeymoon. The two girls were staying at Lucas and Becks'.

I found my eyes sliding back towards the cafe.

Was fifteen years really that much of a difference?

Lucas and Beck's Behind the Scenes look at Their Pregnancy Journey, "Seven Months".

Trevor and Monica's Christmas Novella, "Second Christmas".

Caroline and Nick's age-gap romance in, "Fifteen Years", Book Three of the Finding Freedom series by D. Raven.

Nick and Caroline's Christmas Novella, "Third Christmas".

NEED MORE D. RAVEN?

Check out Lucas and Beck's Story in "Thirteen Years", Book
One of the Finding Freedom series by D. Raven.
Released July 2024.
Also on Audiobook.

Lucas and Beck's Christmas Novella, "First Christmas".
Released December 2024.

Also:

Unsuspecting Valentine: A MaskTok-Meets-BookTok Romance
The Wicked Meet Cute Series by D. Raven
Released February 2025

ACKNOWLEDGEMENTS AND THANK YOUS

Four books? And, did anyone happen to see how many more I have slotted for the series? Plus another that could also branch out into a series? What is happening?!

I can't believe this is real life. SO much has happened since Thirteen Years was written and debuted that I'm terrified I am going to leave someone out of my thank yous and never forgive myself.

Thank you to Izzy Elliott, for making me do this. You helped bring this to fruition. You got my book going and it's in two of the three physical bookstores it's in now because of you! For being my ultimate cheerleader, protector, editor, publisher, PR person, boxer, shipper, best friend, soul sister, and everything else I could ever imagine I would need. I don't know what I did to deserve you, but I'm eternally grateful.

Thank you to Debra Pignol with My Blush Box for reaching out and wanting to place my debut novel in your book box subscription. Then you ran and got my book in a physical book store. THEN you went above and beyond and became a friend who will help me with anything that I ask. You are truly an amazing, wonderful, selfless woman. You and your husband deserve all the good things this life gives you.

Aurelia with Mayonaka Designs, you have taken my babies and made them presentable to the world. I love everything you do and create for them. It's like you go into my head and pluck the information out. I am so grateful you are along for this journey and you are willing to work with my needy self.

To Lindsey Staton (Instagram: Honey.Fae), Lia (Instagram: spicyread_by_lia), and alice.huff_draws1 on Instagram. You all have taken my characters and brought them to life with your beautiful art. I couldn't imagine these beings looking any other way now and I fear you all are stuck with me.

To R.L. Hemm for reaching out to me and telling me you loved my book enough to want to narrate it. For opening me up to possibilities that I didn't think were possible for a little author with a debut novel that hadn't gone anywhere yet. Thank you for bringing these characters to life with audible voices and emotions. Thank you for opening this story up to a whole new audience. I cannot imagine doing this with anyone else now.

To D. Raven's Unkindness Hype Squad - Thank you for loving my books and characters with a passion that still awes me daily. Every share, post, like, comment, and anything else you do for me is beyond inspiring and something I will be eternally grateful for always. You each are special to me and I don't know what I would do or where I would be without you guys.

To my readers. YOU GUYS! I wouldn't be doing this if you hadn't loved Thirteen Years. Any time you DM me, leave a review, comment, ANYTHING I am blown away and humbled by the fact that YOU chose to read my stories and love them. You all are the backbone of an indie author's journey. Without you, each and every single one of you, I wouldn't be doing this. I am forever in your debt.

Remember, YOU are important, YOU deserve good things, and YOU matter.

Love,
D. Raven

ABOUT THE AUTHOR

D. Raven is a single mom of one special needs child. She lives in the Midwest portion of the United States.

Being unable to work due to her child's needs she relies on the kindness of her family and friends a lot. In order to try to earn income herself and pursue a lifelong passion, she started writing

She loves reading, writing, music, and friends. She is a fierce introvert.

You can find her on Instagram, Amazon, and Goodreads.
IG: @author_d_raven
Email: Draven.writesromance@gmail.com
Goodreads: Author D. Raven
Website: www.dravenbooks.com

Her books' Spotify playlists can be found on Spotify at Author_D_Raven

Follow her for more updates and special announcements.

www.ingramcontent.com/pod-product-compliance
Lightning Source LLC
Chambersburg PA
CBHW070419310726
48977CB00003B/760